Equal Danger

BOOKS BY LEONARDO SCIASCIA

Equal Danger
A Man's Blessing

Equal Danger

LEONARDO SCIASCIA

*Translated from the Italian
by Adrienne Foulke*

HARPER & ROW, PUBLISHERS

New York   Evanston   San Francisco   London

Originally published in Italy under the title *Il Contesto*.

EQUAL DANGER. English translation copyright © 1973 by Harper &
Row, Publishers, Inc. All rights reserved. Printed in the United States
of America. No part of this book may be used or reproduced in any
manner whatsoever without written permission except in the case of
brief quotations embodied in critical articles and reviews. For information address Harper & Row, Publishers, Inc., 10 East 53rd Street,
New York, N.Y. 10022. Published simultaneously in Canada by Fitz-
henry & Whiteside Limited, Toronto.

FIRST EDITION

Designed by Patricia Dunbar

Library of Congress Cataloging in Publication Data

Sciascia, Leonardo.
  Equal danger.
  Translation of Il contesto.
  I. Title.
PZ4.S416Eq [PQ4879.C54]   853'.9'14   72-9176
ISBN 0-06-013809-2

One must do as the animals do, who erase every foot-print in front of their lair.

—Montaigne

O Montaigne! You who pride yourself on your candor and truthfulness, be sincere and truthful, if a philosopher can be so, and tell me whether there exists on earth a country where it is a crime to keep one's given word and to be clement and generous, where the good man is despised and the wicked man honored.

—Rousseau

O Rousseau!

—Anonymous

District Attorney Varga was conducting the prosecution in the Reis trial, which had been going on for almost a month and would have dragged on for at least two more, when, one mild May night, after ten and not later than twelve, according to various testimony and to the autopsy, they killed him. The testimony, in point of fact, did not strictly coincide with the results of the autopsy: the medical examiner placed the time of death near midnight, whereas friends with whom the District Attorney, a man of rigid habits, was accustomed to spend every evening, and with whom he had indeed spent that evening, stated that at ten o'clock, give or take a few minutes, he had left them. Since it would not have taken him more than ten minutes to reach his house on foot, there remained the blank of at least one hour, and the need to find out where and how the District Attorney had spent that hour. Perhaps his habits were less fixed than they appeared and there were unprogramed hours in his day, hours of solitary and absent-minded perambulation; perhaps he had habits unknown even to his family and friends. Malicious conjectures were privately expressed and also whispered by the police, on the one hand, by friends on the other;

but to prevent their publicly exploding, the conjectures were promptly defused by a top-level decision reached at a meeting among the highest authorities in the district which branded any suspicion about that pregnant hour as an attack on the memory of a life that henceforth would be reflected in the mirror of all the virtues. The District Attorney had been found at the foot of a low wall from which hung masses of jasmine; he had a flower clasped between his fingers. This moved the bishop to say that in the fatal moment there had been fulfilled the small yet significant destiny of that freshly plucked flower, symbol of an unsullied life, of a goodness still scattering its fragrance in the halls of justice and no less in the bosom of the family and in every place the District Attorney had been accustomed to frequent, the bishop's residence included. This conceit received various elaborations. Police reports suggested that his pausing to pluck the jasmine had offered the criminal a precise target (a single shot, straight to the heart, fired from a distance of six or eight feet). Eulogies delivered at the funeral averred that the act of plucking the little flower bespoke a delicacy of feeling and a penchant for poetry which, for that matter, had never been belied by Varga, either in the exercise of his calling or in his private conduct. At one point in his oration, the pedantic Mr. Siras quoted, with a groan, *"avisad los jazmines con su blancura pequeña"*—"warn the jasmine with its tiny whiteness"— in his grief forgetting that, given the incontestable auricular faculties of jasmine, the blossoms had got the news instantly from a gun blast which the experts estimated had been quite heavy, as well as from the lawyer's last breath, whereas several hours passed before the police were alerted, by which time at least a third of the city's inhabitants had contemplated the corpse.

The Reis trial was suspended. And since District Attorney Varga had conducted the prosecution with implacable acumen, the police believed one should look to the trial for the motive that had armed the hand of the unknown assassin. Nowhere in the nation's history of crime, or at least nowhere in the experience of the investigators, were there precedents of the kind; never had prosecutors or judges been threatened or struck down for a position taken during a trial or for a verdict delivered. However, considering that the Reis case was based entirely on circumstantial evidence and offered impenetrable obscurities of feelings and facts, the suspicion that someone had wished to silence Varga's inexorable prosecution, or wished merely to muddy the already sufficiently muddied waters of the affair, was deemed promising by the police. But relatives and friends of the defendant (the friends numbering very few at the moment) proved to be above or beneath suspicion. Accordingly, the police proceeded to his enemies, attributing to them a twisted and diabolic design not only to make the misdeeds of the accused appear unchallengeable but also to implicate other persons whom the pretrial examining judges had believed should be left on the sidelines. But even in this area the detectives' chase ended in failure.

Investigations having led to a dead end—i.e., to that hour or more the District Attorney had spent who knows where and how, a dim zone at the boundaries of which the zeal of the police was forcibly curbed—the authorities acted. Whether to restore to public opinion a faith in the efficiency of the police that, as it happens, public opinion had never nourished, or to make the public accept the unsolvability of the mystery, the Minister for National Security decided to assign Inspector Rogas to the case: the shrewdest investigator at the disposal of the police, according to the newspapers; the luckiest, in the judgment of his colleagues. The Minister did not fail to communicate to Rogas, by way of a viaticum delivered by the High Commissioner of Police, the desire of both the President of the Supreme Court and himself that any shadow which might blemish the limpid reputation of the deceased Varga should be evaluated by Rogas in light of the discredit that would unjustly fall upon the entire judiciary; therefore, with the utmost caution, any such shadow was to be exorcised upon its first appearance. Should it loom up irresistibly, it was to be erased. But Rogas had principles, in a country where almost no one did. Therefore, immediately but alone and with discretion, he pushed on into the forbidden zone, and he would have emerged—like a dog who comes out from the vapors of a swamp, the coot between his jaws—bearing who knows what snippet of Varga's reputation, had he not been stopped short by the news that Judge Sanza had been found dead on the beach at Ales (a pistol shot to the heart).

Ales was about sixty miles from the city where Rogas was checking into the assassination of Varga, but he could not go there without the permission of his chief. He requested it by telephone; he received it by letter. He arrived in Ales three days later, when the local police had already arrested a dozen people who had nothing whatever to do with the case but from among whom the police

4

were all agog to draw the guilty one virtually by lot. Rogas made a brief study of the motives attributed to those under arrest; the motives were such that only if fueled by madness could they have brought anyone to plan and carry out a murder. Since none of the twelve men appeared mad, whereas Inspector Magris, who commanded the local constabulary, *was* a bit mad, Rogas had them released. After which, having settled himself into the best hotel in town, on the magnificent beach where during his solitary walk Judge Sanza had met death, Rogas gave himself over to an indolence that verged on the ostentatious and bordered on the scandalous. He swam, he went out with the fishermen in their boats, he dined on the catch at its freshest, he slept hours on end. Inspector Magris hovered around him frantically, humiliated to have to be subordinate to someone who was equal to him in rank and superior to him in prestige; although full of bitterness, at the same time Magris savored the failure his colleague was heading toward, the brusque recall to the capital, the derision of the press.

However, Rogas's head was working. Two major public officials murdered within the space of one week, in two cities not very far from each other, in the same manner, with bullets of the same caliber fired perhaps from the same weapon (he never relied on reports from police laboratories to contain hard facts). He considered there was enough at hand to work on the hypothesis of a revenge that an unjustly condemned man might have vowed to carry out against his prosecutor, against his judges. Except that District Attorney Varga and Judge Sanza had never, at any point in their careers, been associated in the same trial; this fact Rogas had readily confirmed upon learning of the second crime. Yet the hypothesis held up. Rogas found reasons for not abandoning it: (1) The murderer could have been found guilty first in a court where Varga was conducting the prosecution, and later in a court where Sanza shared the bench with fellow-judges. Or it could have been the reverse—Sanza functioning in the lower, Varga in the appellate court. (2) The murderer could have made a mistake in the case of one of his two victims because of erroneous information, a lapse of memory, a case of homonyms (phonogram: IS THERE, HAS THERE EVER BEEN ANOTHER DISTRICT ATTORNEY VARGA, ANOTHER JUDGE SANZA?), for, as everybody knows, entire families have dedicated themselves, generation after generation, to certain public offices. (3) The murderer could have deliberately sought to confuse things, to make his game indecipherable, his identity impenetrable, by killing one of the two gratuitously, either the lawyer or the Judge (phonogram: WHO FROM AMONG THOSE SENTENCED IN TRIALS IN WHICH VARGA AND SANZA TOOK PART HAS LEFT PRISON IN THE LAST SIX MONTHS?). However, out of a superstitious attachment to the number three, which he considered characteristic of the neuroses of others as well as of his own, Rogas was convinced that there would be a third victim, and that it would be the good one; that is, the one that would turn up the clue necessary for him to solve the problem. As it presented itself at the moment, the problem was insoluble. And so Rogas was waiting. The third victim glowed in his mind, trespassing into the realms of yearning and fantasy, like an abstract sign that was on the verge of becoming name, body, funeral, inheritance, pension, and, above all, the element with which to advance the investigation on some basis firmer than thin air.

He did not have to wait long. Four days later, in Chiro, Judge Azar was felled: a sullen, reclusive man, who had spent the years from youth to death in terror of being infected by illnesses and emotions. Never had he shaken hands with a colleague or with a lawyer; when he could not avoid shaking hands because some newly arrived superior offered his own, Azar would suffer until he managed to slink behind a curtain or to some place where he, not seeing, believed himself unseen; taking out a tiny flask of alcohol, he would pour a generous amount (the only thing in which he was generous) over his bony hands, which were roped with veins and spotted like lichen-covered stones. Yet in his funeral eulogy, the highest-ranking magistrate in Chiro must perforce invent the wealth of human kindness that Azar concealed beneath a rough and callused hide. The other wealth, the real wealth, was discovered by the son of a sister, the Judge's only heir. Having rushed to Chiro upon receiving news of his uncle's tragic end, he would have remained who knows how long a guest in the local jail had Rogas not arrived to set him free. The young man, somewhat dissolute, had no alibi for the evening Azar had been murdered, and although by now it was clear to everyone that somebody, whether seeking revenge or simply mad, was running around murdering judges, the police did not renounce the almost ritual habit of swiftly, even joyously, sacrificing the reputation of persons who were the last to see a murdered man alive or who stood to gain by his death.

Having won the nephew's confidence, Rogas, as if to help him, and actually being helpful, kept after the young man to make an inventory of the estate. It turned out to be worth a sum at least twenty times larger than the amount the State had paid the Judge in salary over twenty-two years, assuming that in twenty-two years the Judge had spent not one penny for food, lodging, clothing, and disinfectants. Nor, insofar as the nephew could recall, had the Judge begun his career owning anything; on the contrary, the young man had been forever hearing from his mother the exemplary tale of the privations and the hunger against which her brother, now a judge of high rank and incorruptible prestige, had struggled in his younger years. Accordingly, Rogas began to inquire into that fortune, convinced that even if the investigation would not prove useful in uncovering the reason for which Azar had been murdered, it would surely provide some clue to what kind of judge he had been.

But Rogas, acting on the hypothesis of Azar's corruptibility, had no sooner begun to bestir himself, to speak with this or that person, to solicit confidences, than there arrived from the capital an authoritative exhortation not to forage for gossip; Rogas should keep on the trail, if trail there was, of that crazy lunatic who for no reason whatever was going about murdering judges. The crazy-lunatic thesis had by now come into favor at the very top levels: the Minister for Security, the Minister for Justice, the President of the Supreme Court, the High Commissioner of Police. Even the President of the Republic, Rogas's boss informed him confidentially, was asking every morning whether the homicidal madman had been caught. So far, and Rogas was astonished at this, the affair had not been tossed into the political arena, not even by those papers that were always ready to attribute every senseless or monstrous crime to one of the many revolutionary groups that swarmed throughout the country.

Luckily, before Rogas could register disagreement with his superior's directives, the information he had requested immediately on learning of Azar's death did arrive: for about two years, Azar and Varga had served in the Criminal Court in Algo. Rogas abruptly disappeared from Chiro, just as he had disappeared from Ales. Newsmen lost track of him until a local correspondent reported his presence in Algo. Thereupon, the most disparate conjectures were bandied about, and they grew positively wild when, right in Algo, Judge Rasto was killed. Had Rogas known that the assassin would fell his fourth victim in Algo? And if he knew, why on earth had he not managed to prevent the crime? Had he made a lucky guess? Had he prepared a trap for the assassin? If so, the trap had not worked, and to bait it with a judge was a bit too much. *The Fuse,* a newspaper whose editors had impartial faith in violent social rebirth and in the equally violent adverse powers of the evil eye, insinuated that Rogas possessed innate malefic gifts. This insinuation, passing from the paper's few readers to the many who did not read it, became a certitude, so that at the mention of the name "Rogas" at least two-thirds of the adult population of the country knocked on wood and stroked good-luck charms for the better part of a week. At the end of which time, fearing that the attribution of fatal powers might be extended to the entire police corps and to the very Ministry he headed, the Minister for

9

Security hastily summoned newsmen to explain the intentions of the police and of Rogas and, above all, to clarify the reason for the Inspector's presence in Algo only shortly before Judge Rasto was killed. Rogas, he explained, had gone to Algo on the strength of a clue he had managed to uncover, the only clue that somehow connected two of the three murders committed to that point: ten years ago, Varga and Azar had served for about two years in the Criminal Court in Algo. Now, the fact that the unknown assassin had struck again, in Algo, was to be explained by the papers' having published news of Rogas's presence in the city, and, accordingly, was to be understood as a challenge hurled at the police, a challenge the police accepted; on the basis of the clue discovered by Rogas, they were hard at work tracking down the homicidal madman.

The Minister's statements made Rogas so nervous that he telephoned his chief begging to be relieved of the assignment if the Minister was really determined to put a spoke in the wheels. His chief comforted him and ordered him to go on with his investigation. But, as Rogas feared, the assassin's reply to the Minister came promptly: in a city far, far from Algo, Judge Calamo fell —a man who, as far as could be immediately learned, had had no connection with any of the other four victims. Which meant one of several possible things: the murderer had killed Judge Rasto according to plan, unaware of Rogas's presence; or he had known of Rogas's presence and had wanted to challenge him; or he now realized he had made a false step, a mistake, and was trying to lure the Inspector away from Algo and from the clue he had discovered there, drawing him into a labyrinth of counterfeit clues.

But Rogas did not stir from Algo. He had assembled the records of all the trials in which Varga as prosecutor and Azar as judge had taken part, and after a summary examination he divided and regrouped them according to simple criteria. A first group, nineteen trials that had ended with a verdict of not guilty, he eliminated immediately. The second group, thirty-five trials in which the defendants had been found guilty either because they had confessed or because they had been apprehended by the police in the act of committing the crimes or because the evidence and proofs were incontestable, he also eliminated after carefully examining four cases that, in the police reports or in the statements of witnesses, seemed to him to strike some false note. He returned the fifty-four eliminated trial records to the court archives, and retained a group of twenty-two in which the accused had been found guilty on the basis of assumptions and circumstantial evidence but had always, throughout police interrogations, pretrial examinations, and trial proceedings, protested their innocence.

Rogas made a list of those in the twenty-two trials who had been sentenced. It was complete in every detail that might serve to track them down. He distributed the list to judicial and police offices that were in a position to know the fate of those persons, whether they were still in prison or had left. In this way, he learned that fourteen of the men were still in prison; eight had regained their freedom, either because they had served their sentences or had had them reduced for good conduct or by amnesties, or because they had been found innocent upon appeal. Rogas concentrated for more than a week on these eight men and the documents relating to their trials. It was a kind of escape, a kind of game for him. He extracted from the documents the elements that could have been used to prove the innocence of the defendants. It gave him a sense of freedom, it amused him to skirt or suppress reactions of his own that, conditioned by habit and professional experience, continually suggested guilt.

In all eight cases, according to Rogas, the elements that could have persuaded the judges to find the defendants innocent prevailed over those they had used to justify a verdict of guilty, a conviction. And supremely unjust, it seemed to him, was the element of "previous acts of misconduct," as in the phrase "demonstrated tendency toward delinquency," which in five out of the eight cases was accepted as an incontrovertible, definitive argument. If someone had stolen some plums from a neighbor's orchard when he was twelve, it was assumed that at thirty he could very well kill with intent to rob. And if he had stolen those plums from a canonical orchard, it was entirely credible that ten years later he would be capable of murdering his mother. And so on and so on, with "previous acts of misconduct" being constantly referred to—and this in a country which boasted a whole body of literature dealing with the unforeseeable moods, contradictions, gratuitous actions, and radical changes to which human beings are prone. But while Rogas considered that attaching importance to "previous acts of misconduct" was an offense and an impediment to justice, he lingered longest over three

12

cases in which the protagonists had committed no such "previous acts," and it was with these three cases that his on-the-spot investigation began.

The three persons lived in the district of Algo. Their cases, upon appeal by defense or prosecution, had moved up from one level to another of the judicial hierarchy until, after a period of years (rather long years if measured within the cell of a prison, brief as a puff of air in the sidereal course steered by the administration of justice in the country), the cases had finally reached the Supreme Court. Here doubt, not about the facts on the basis of which these men had been found guilty but about the application of the law that had condemned them, had become manifest to the judges; the defendants had been remanded for new trials. The results: one had had his sentence confirmed; one had had his increased by two years; one had been cleared. Rogas began with the last man, because it seemed to him that, both for reasons of the man's character as it emerged from the proceedings and for the very fact of his being finally absolved, he was the one to be ruled out immediately.

The man had neither a fixed residence nor an occupation. Not that he had been ruined by the trial and the four years he had spent in prison; on the contrary, his troubles had come from a vocation to laziness that he flaunted, considering it a design of Providence. Since, as everyone knows, laziness is the father of every vice, to the police and to the judges in the court of first instance it had seemed in order to charge him with homicide with intent to rob. There were no "previous acts of misconduct," but there was laziness.

Rogas found him in the square, seated in the sun at the

13

foot of a monument to a General Carco who, a hundred years earlier, had freed the region from one tyranny only to impose another on it. The man had pulled his beret down over his eyes. He sat motionless, in a position of total abandonment. Perhaps he was asleep. Rogas stopped in front of him, to cast a shadow over him. As if in play, he lifted the man's beret. A disgusted, questioning glance fixed him. So the man was not asleep. Then a shadow of suspicion passed through his eyes. Rogas saw himself being brought into focus, recognized for what he was. Without shifting position, apparently relaxed, the man was now tense, watchful.

"How are things going?" the Inspector asked. The tone sought to be, and was, cordial; nonetheless it was a question, the beginning of an inquisition.

"They're not," the man said.

"What's wrong?"

"Everything."

"And before?"

"Before what?"

"Before, I mean, things went all right?"

"Never."

"So then?"

"So then here I am."

"All the time?"

"Not all the time. Sometimes I sit in the square by the market, sometimes at the café."

"A little trip somewhere?"

"I'd like that. But the last one I took was to Rus. Seven miles, on foot. Three years ago."

"What's your hunch about these judges being murdered?" Rogas spoke to him familiarly because the fel-

14

low was the type that expected old-buddy treatment from the authorities even if they were being ruthless.

"I'm sorry about them," the man said, like someone who knows he is giving an unsatisfactory answer and meanwhile is feverishly preparing more satisfactory responses to the questions to come. He was moving from tension into fear.

"District Attorney Varga—" Rogas began.

"He seemed convinced that I'd killed that shopkeeper. He talked well, he was convincing. He wanted them to give me thirty years. He was sorry, he said, that there was no death penalty anymore."

"And Judge Azar?"

"He gave me twenty-seven. Not all by himself, though. There were two other judges."

"I know. And they're still alive. And you?"

"What could *I* do? I rolled with the punches. I was lucky the court assigned me a young lawyer who wanted to make a name for himself. He appealed, carried my case right up to the Supreme Court. And now here I am."

"And those four years in jail?"

"Over and done with."

"Over and done with, all right. But you did four years unjustly, didn't you?"

"I've done fifty-two years of life unjustly. Actually, the four I spent in jail don't bother me much. Prison is safe."

"Safe how?"

"For eating, sleeping. Everything's regulated for you."

"And freedom?"

"Freedom is here," the man said, pressing a finger against the middle of his forehead.

15

"But you said you'd been lucky to find a lawyer who got you out of jail."

"It's a manner of speaking. Sure, it wasn't bad luck. They said I'd killed a man to take his money. The lawyer proved I was innocent; that's good luck. But as for the rest . . ." With his hand, he made a gesture of dismissal, of indifference.

Rogas rested a hand on his shoulder, by way of saying goodbye. He walked away. Turning when he reached the edge of the square, he saw that the man had again tipped his beret over his eyes and had resumed his relaxed position. Sun. Rest, idleness. The dignity of rest, the civilization of idleness. Luis Cernuda, *Variaciones sobre tema mexicana.* Fine book. "Freedom is here." Well, no; in the end, they don't leave you even that.

For the second man, on the other hand, things were going very well, at least as the world judges such matters. He owned a machine shop, he worked night and day. He was making money, and this money he invested in a flourishing trade in new and secondhand cars. But maybe things were going better for the first man, Rogas reflected when he saw the second man come out, sweaty and covered with grease, from under an automobile he was repairing.

He did not realize that Rogas was from the police. He said he was busy; a car belonging to some American tourists had to be repaired immediately. He couldn't imagine what urgency there could be about the interview Rogas was asking for.

"Police. Inspector Rogas."

The grease and sweat became a mask on the man's

suddenly ashen face. "All right," he said. "Let's go in there." They went into a little glass-walled room. There were two chairs; he motioned for Rogas to take one; he fell into his like a puppet whose strings have been cut, disarticulated, lifeless. Then, groping, he felt for his cigarettes on the table, lighted one, staring at the Inspector with eyes that seemed to be looking out from behind a wall, from within a cave. His hands shook.

"I'm here just for a little checkup. No doubt it will be useless, but in our work to move ahead you must first clear the ground of superfluous things, useless things; otherwise you end up finding them in the way when you least expect them. . . . For example, when I came in here I realized immediately that it would be difficult for you to leave your shop for a day or even just for a few hours without your workmen and customers not only noticing your absence, and remembering it, but also asking for explanations and excuses. 'The boss is not here?' 'He's sick.' . . . 'He's gone to a wedding.' . . . 'He's been called down to the tax bureau.' . . . 'And when will he be back?' . . . In other words, your being away can't help but be noticed."

"It can't help but be noticed," the mechanic said, a bit reassured.

"But you've understood why I've come to see you?" Rogas asked.

"I think so."

"So tell me. In the last weeks, have you been away from here for periods of, say, hours or days that would reasonably allow you to have got as far as places like Ales, Chiro—"

"No, absolutely not."

17

"—and in connection," Rogas continued, "with the murders of District Attorney Varga and Judges Sanza, Azar, Rasto?"

"As I said, no, absolutely not."

"But you remember District Attorney Varga? Judge Azar?"

"I dream about them at night," and he brushed his hand over his face like someone who is emerging from a dream and wants to wipe any recollection of it away.

"You think of yourself as their victim?"

"Not exactly their victim. A victim."

"What effect does it have on you to know that they've been murdered?"

"None. It was the system. I got caught in the system. It could have done me in. Instead I got out alive."

"But you were innocent!"

"Do you really believe that?"

"I'm here because I believe it."

"Yes, I was innocent. . . . But what does it mean to be innocent when you get caught in the wheels of the system? It doesn't mean a thing, I can tell you. Not even to me, at a certain point. Like crossing a street, and a car runs you down. You're innocent, and you're run down by a car. What sense is there in such a thing?"

"But not everybody is innocent," Rogas said. "I mean, not all the people who get caught in the wheels of the system."

"The way the system works, they could all be innocent."

"But then you could also say, as far as innocence goes, that we could all get caught in the wheels of the system."

"Perhaps. But I'm not a Party man, so I put it differently."

Rogas thought, He knows how to develop an idea, how to reach a conclusion quickly. And he added cynically, Prison did him good. Aloud, he said, "I understand." He resumed his professional tone of voice. "And so, in these last days, you have not left your work even for a day; you have not gone out of town—"

"Sunday the shop is closed, naturally. But I'm here, taking care of the books, putting everything in order. And if someone comes in with a small repair job, I don't say no."

"Sunday . . ." Rogas said. None of the crimes he was investigating had occurred on a Sunday. "And evenings during the work week? How do you spend your evenings?"

"I close up after ten and go to the restaurant."

"Which one?"

"The Hunter."

"Every evening?"

"Every evening. I live alone."

"Why?"

"You read the transcript of my trial?"

"Yes, I read it. I see." He stood up. "I must warn you that I will have to check on your evenings at the Hunter."

"I'm sorry about that because people will start talking about me again, my case, new suspicions the police have about me. But what can I do? It's the system."

"I'll try to do it discreetly, tactfully."

"Thank you."

Rogas left the Hunter at three in the afternoon. He had had an excellent lunch, half a wild rabbit in sweet-and-sour sauce, a bottle of red wine, full-bodied, with a just discernible trace of jasmine in it, and he had verified the mechanic's alibi beyond any shadow of doubt. He felt satisfied, confident, both because he belonged to the ever more numerous ranks of those who celebrate and rejoice in wild game, home-grown fruit, homemade bread, and a simple table wine as relics from the golden age, and because it seemed to him that in the person he was now going to seek out were crystallized the ideal elements of the capacity to commit a kind of ideal crime. The process of crystallization, not dissimilar to that of love (Stendhal, *De l'amour*), had taken place in Rogas as he read and reread the trial records, talked with all the people who had had something to do with the case, and collected the most minute information about the protagonist.

The facts, as related to him by his colleague Contrera, who had been in charge of the inspectorate in Algo, were these (but they were not facts only; they spilled over into impressions, judgments): on the evening of October 25, 1958, a Mrs. Cres appears at the inspectorate. She asks to speak with the Inspector. The officer on duty and, subsequently, the Inspector note that she is upset, agitated, frightened. The woman is carrying a parcel, cylindrical in shape. She undoes it; out comes a small enameled pot; the woman takes off the lid and pushes the pot under the Inspector's nose. The Inspector looks at it: a granular, chocolate-colored pulp.

"Black rice," the woman says.

20

"What?" the Inspector asks.

"Rice with chocolate," the woman explains. "Have you never eaten it?"

"Never."

"I like it so much."

"It probably is good," the Inspector says, and he begins to feel a slight apprehension.

"Yes, but not this," the woman says.

"Why not?" the Inspector asks, feigning interest as if he were playing a child's game. "Is there something wrong with this rice?"

"It's poisoned," the woman says, terrified and solemn.

"Oh, poisoned," the Inspector says to keep up the game, convinced that he is dealing with a madwoman. "And who has poisoned it?"

"I don't know," the woman says, "but the cat's dead."

"Oh, the cat . . . And who had any reason to kill the cat?"

"No one, I think. But I was the one who gave the black rice to the cat."

"So it was you. Why?"

"Because I didn't know it was poisoned."

"Tell me everything in order," the Inspector says. He thinks, Either a story is going to come out that will have to be transcribed for the record or it's a case of calling the ambulance. But from the woman's last response, his conviction that she is crazy is beginning to waver. In fact, the woman relates her story coherently.

Her husband is a pharmacist, and she helps him in the pharmacy. Rather, they spell each other, for now doctors rarely write out prescriptions in the old way—so much of this and so much of that—and with the nonprescription

21

medicines she works with greater dispatch than her husband because she has a better memory. When she comes down to the pharmacy, her husband goes upstairs to their living quarters or goes out to his club for a game of billiards. Most often he goes upstairs, because he loves to cook, and to tell the truth, some things he cooks to perfection. Black rice, for example—how he can cook that. . . . And she is a glutton for it. Now, that very day the pharmacist had prepared black rice. When he had returned to the pharmacy, he had said nothing to her; it had been a surprise for her to find the black rice in the kitchen, in the form of a conch shell, black and shining on the flowered serving dish. It was fragrant with cinnamon, perhaps a little too much cinnamon. Ordinarily she cannot resist tasting it and then serving herself a portion. But that day she had had an inspiration, surely heaven-sent. The cat had followed her upstairs from the pharmacy, where he habitually stayed; he was meowing, his whiskers trembled at the perfume of the cinnamon, and she—like that, impulsively—had taken a spoonful of black rice and given it to him right there, on the floor.

"Why?" the Inspector asked. "Why on the floor?" His wife would never have done that; she grew angry when the children dropped a tiny bite of meat for the cat who was under the table. (Thanks to his wife, Rogas reflected, his colleague Contrera had asked the only sensible question in the entire investigation.)

"But I told you—like that, impulsively, a kind of inspiration."

"I don't believe in impulses that conflict with habits, and much less in divine inspiration," the Inspector said.

"Wasn't there something that aroused your suspicions and made you act like that?"

"Maybe the overstrong smell of cinnamon."

"Well-l-l," the Inspector said, loading his doubt with two or three "l"s. "Anyhow, let's go on. What about the cat?"

"The cat ate the spoonful of black rice with gusto, licked the floor clean, and looked up, meowing and waiting for a second helping. Then suddenly he shrank; he seemed to withdraw into himself, puffing like a little organ. . . . But the bit about the organ occurs to me just now. At the time, he made me think of the sleeve of an empty fur coat that goes through the motions of turning inside out all by itself. . . . Then he leaped up like a spring and fell down on his side, stretched full length and stiff on the floor."

"And you?"

"I was frightened to death. But I kept myself from crying out."

"Why?"

"I don't know about why then. Now, having collected my wits, I can say that perhaps it was a flash of suspicion."

"The suspicion that only your husband could have put some poison in the whatchamacallit?"

"In the black rice," the woman corrected him, and she did not reply to the question. She was very calm now. A beautiful woman, between thirty and forty, the Inspector had noted; a vibrant, restless body.

"But why did you think of poison?"

"What else could I think of?"

"Cats can perfectly well die the way people often die. On the street, chewing a mouthful of food, lighting a cigarette —"

"The smoking cat," the woman said, with half a smile. "Excuse me, in my mind's eye, I just saw the sign of a Paris café."

"It's a dog—Le Chien Qui Fume," the Inspector said, irritated. "In any event, a cat can die suddenly, too. He finishes eating the black rice, and he dies. How is it you haven't thought your cat might have happened to die suddenly?"

"I don't know; perhaps because for some time I've not been sure my husband loves me."

"Loves you? But between not being sure your husband loves you and being certain, all of a sudden, that your husband meant to kill you with the black rice, there is, I'd say, a big difference."

"I've never said anything about being certain. I'm talking about impressions, presentiments, fears. Certainty must come from analyses. I've brought you the black rice, and the cat, too; I put it in a bag in the trunk of the car. And there is no point in going on about my impressions before one knows the results of the tests. To you I say simply this: I believe someone wanted to make an attempt on my life, but who I don't know. If the cat is really dead from poison, if there is poison in the black rice . . ."

The cat was dead from poison; in the rice there was enough to kill a dozen people. The pharmacist did not deny having prepared the dessert; he excluded the possibility that anyone other than his wife could have added poison to the sweet. A check showed that the quantity of poison found in the dessert was precisely the amount that, according to the register, was missing from the pharmacy supply; and on the glass jar there were only the fingerprints of the pharmacist. The envelope in which the poison had been put was found in the pocket of his dressing gown (he put on his dressing gown when he was acting as cook), and in his wallet was found (a serious clue) a very brief letter that seemed to have been written by his wife (the experts found the handwriting well imitated but denied its authenticity): "I can live no longer. You have nothing to do with it. It is not your fault, so feel no remorse. Live in peace."

Missing was a motive, apart from the woman's vague impressions as to the diminishing of his love for her (never did she allow another expression to pass her lips, and with intransigent modesty rejected every allusion to sexual relations). However, when something is lacking, God provides, and an anonymous letter arrived opportunely to supply a precious clue: ten days, two weeks before, the pharmacist had stopped by the house of a local whore; he had told her some things in confidence. The lady, having been summoned to police headquarters, did not require much working over to confess the secret that the pharmacist had confided in her: he had a "cold" wife. The Inspector did not find it plausible that a husband would try to do away with his wife because she was "cold"; the motive was not serious—after all, all women are "cold." But he took note of the whore's confession and passed it along, without embellishing it by so much as a word, to the pretrial judge, whose dreams, at the side of a "cold" woman, were populated with "hot" women. Accordingly, the effects of the coldness that Mrs.

Cres exhibited with regard to her consort became the basis on which District Attorney Varga and Judge Azar and company built up a sentence of five years for attempted homicide, which sentence was confirmed by the appellate court then presided over by Judge Riches, who subsequently moved up to preside over the Supreme Court.

In the course of his trial, defended by a lawyer by no means convinced of his innocence, pharmacist Cres maintained an attitude that seemed disdainful. He said that in the light of common sense nothing prevented his accusers, or his judges, from thinking that the whole affair might be the machination of his wife. The appeal to good sense irritated the District Attorney and the presiding judges. The District Attorney asked him if his wife was attached to the cat. The pharmacist conceded her affection. "Very much attached?" District Attorney Varga insinuated. Cres replied that he was unable to establish the degree of affection, and added ironically, "She seemed to be attached to me, too." An appeal to good sense, irony—things an accused man must never permit himself. Varga delivered a tirade against the defendant's cynicism, and concluded with the declaration: "And therefore, even admitting that the lady might have been capable of conceiving and carrying out such a diabolic design (yet why, since not even her husband has managed to point to a motive), is it thinkable that she would have gone to such lengths as to sacrifice the innocent creature to which, by the admission of the person who would wish to saddle *her* with the charge that pinches him, she was so greatly attached?" Whispers of indignation, of incredulity, serpentined through the courtroom; the lady president of the Society for the Protection of Animals, present at every session both in her official capacity and as a friend of Mrs. Cres, cried out "Impossible!" and the defense lawyer turned to the pharmacist with a gesture that meant their case was irremediably lost.

After the appeal, Mrs. Cres disappeared. Without warning, without even saying goodbye to the women friends who had been so close to her for the duration of the wretched case. For all they knew at the police station, she could even have been dead. But at that point Inspector Contrera had a theory of his own. During the trial, he had already had some suspicions; nothing factual, one must understand, only the suspicion that in that concatenation of clues there was something contrived, and that of the two, in their loveless life together, the boredom—the desperate, limpid boredom—was more on her side than on her husband's. When, later, Contrera learned that she had disappeared, suspicions fed his theory: the woman had plotted that crime, leaving it up to the police and the judges to execute it, as it were, by filling in the blanks, and she had done so in order to be quit of her husband for as long as it would take her to disappear. Since a woman, according to Contrera, never disappears alone, there must be some man whom the lady had managed, before and after, to keep in the most secret, most impenetrable shadow. Whereupon Contrera made an attempt to turn up something on the woman's score, but without results.

Having served five years, the pharmacist returned home. He did not expect, naturally, to find his wife sitting by the hearth, nor did he bother to learn where she might have gone. He liquidated the pharmacy, sold everything he possessed except for the building, in which he still lived. The house was very dear to him, despite sad memories of the black rice, the cat, the years he had spent there with his wife—years that now, in every remembered image, must appear to him in the cold and sinister light of betrayal. He left the house rarely, rarely sought the company of the two or three friends with whom he had once played billiards and who, invariably of an evening, used to stop by the pharmacy for a summary of the day's happenings.

Rogas, before leaving the restaurant, had made sure that Cres was at home. For three days, with an unobtrusiveness that was facilitated by there being a café opposite, a medieval castle in ruins on one side, and the residence of a brigadier on the other, Cres's house had been assiduously kept under surveillance. He was there. As late as the evening before, toward nightfall, they had seen him walk out onto the balcony in a dressing gown. (Maybe he was preparing black rice, Rogas thought.) Lights burning until past midnight. After which, until now, no sign that he was at home. But he was.

When Rogas arrived, the stakeout gave an almost imperceptible nod to confirm that Cres was there. Rogas searched for a doorbell. There was none. He lifted the lion-head knocker, let it fall. From the empty reverberations in the entrance hall, from the wave of more intense silence that overwhelmed them, Rogas had a presentiment that Cres had gone away. But he continued to pound, louder and louder, with the knocker. Then he

28

turned toward his watchdog, called him over with a wave of his hand. The man came on the run, clutching the glass of ginger beer with which he had been regaling himself. He said, with a mixture of rage and amazement, "He's got to be there!" and fell to pounding in a frenetic crescendo.

"That's enough," Rogas said, for the situation was beginning to look ridiculous to the habitués of the café.

"It was to be expected," Rogas said, and he was not talking about Cres but about the men who for three days had been keeping Cres under surveillance and who had orders to stop him if he tried to get away. It was not the first time; it would not be the last.

"He's got to be inside. Maybe he's asleep, maybe he wants to make us think he's not there," the policeman said.

"It could be," Rogas said, out of pure kindness to the distracted man, who was gasping and breathless, like a runner nearing the post.

"What'll we do?" the policeman asked.

"You go back to the café," Rogas said. "I'll come tonight with a search warrant and a locksmith." He went off, careful not to look in the direction of the spectators.

Cres had gone. Clearly, he had become aware of the surveillance and, at some moment when the man on duty had turned away, he had tranquilly walked out of his house. In two days, he had had time to study the habits of his surveillants; on the third day, he was in a position to carry out his flight. It did not call for much, after all; it was almost a tradition with the police to allow persons under surveillance at any distance to escape. On the surface, the phenomenon suggested an inveterate and

29

widespread negligence; in reality, it had a more danger-
ous root—the inability of police agents and of their superiors to conceive of the existence of an individual who
was to be kept under surveillance and not to be arrested.
The prescribed structure of the police had been, until
only a few years before, purely repressive; that psychol-
ogy, that habit, endured.

But while saying to himself that it was to be expected,
Rogas felt a searing disappointment at not having found
Cres, both because his fellow had walked off with perfect
composure from a house that could have been well
staked out even by a blind man and because the flight,
if flight it was, would complicate matters. Perhaps it was
not a flight. One could not exclude the possibility that
Cres had been aware of nothing, that he had simply gone
off without any plan, without any precautions, under the
very nose of the plainclothesman who, in the oppressive
hallucination of the midday heat, between the snare of
drowsiness and the solace of a cold drink, had forgotten
why he'd been hanging around the café for hours and
had come to see in the man he was supposed to be
watching merely someone leaving his house to go about
his own business or to get some fresh air on the town
ramparts. And there was a still more serious considera-
tion: not all the people who took to their heels when
favored by the attention of the police could be accounted
guilty. On the contrary. In Rogas's experience, there
were more flights of innocent than of guilty people. The
guilty would often sit tight until the attention of the
police took the tangible form of a warrant for arrest,
sometimes impatiently even going so far as to confess,
thereby crossing over the police domain to the more

secure, more reliable terrain of the judicial realm where even confessions required proof and proof was almost always lacking. It was the innocent who took flight. Not all, of course. And an innocent person, someone like Cres, would have good cause to flee. Innocent, perhaps —in any event, convicted on the basis of weak evidence, he had been caught up in the police and judicial system. Five years later, he had come out of it without even the satisfaction that an appellate court, although it would not recognize his innocence, at least had taken cognizance of how inadequate were the proofs of his guilt.

Whether Cres had been unfairly convicted Rogas was not sure. Had he been in the place of his colleague Contrera, who had investigated the case and delivered Cres over to the judges—washing his hands of him, like Pilate—Rogas would have been sure of Cres's guilt or innocence, and with discreet but tenacious insinuation he would have judiciously seeded the reasons for his certainty into his reports. For Rogas, having the man before him, talking with him, getting to know him, counted more than clues—more than facts. "A fact is an empty sack." One had to put the man, the person, the character inside the sack for it to hold up. What kind of man was this Cres, sentenced to five years for attempted homicide, with the aggravating circumstances of premeditation and base motives? What kind of man had he become after his conviction, during the five years in prison, during the other five in which, having returned to freedom, he had lived in his own house almost as if it were a prison? Rogas could only imagine, fantasize. And the most tenable point he had reached, while imagining and fantasizing, was this: Cres was a man who had a kind

31

of vocation for prison; he had made his life into one long prison sentence. One of the most fateful professions a man can choose. And Cres had chosen it at eighteen, barely out of school. He had chosen freely, not because of tradition or family pressure, for his father had been a lawyer and would have liked him to take up the study of law.

Then there was the life he had led, his habits, his pastimes. And a "cold" woman beside him. He had made a prison for himself and, it appeared, was comfortable in it. Therefore, the discovery of a prison in which he could be held unjustly, by force, by violence, through the machinations and decisions of others, had kindled in him a lucid and implacable hatred, a cold and deadly madness. After all, the greatest affirmation of freedom in life is made by the man who creates a prison for himself. (Rogas was contradicting himself.) Montaigne, Kant. Why laugh at poor Cres, at his name being placed side by side with such names as these? Why ridicule Cres if Beethoven, from heaven, from the castle of illustrious spirits, decrees that a perfect performance of his A-Minor Quartet should reach the ears of some English schoolgirls, yet they hear only the murmur of a sea shell, the fanfare of a regiment? The author of this anecdote of Beethovian fantasy, E. M. Forster, called these phenomena "the central sources" of melody, of victory, of thought. (Rogas preferred the term *"res nullius."*) Austerlitz on a picnic. Beethoven in a sea shell. The *Critique of Pure Reason* on a billiard table. The Montaigne *Essays* in pharmacy jars. But the real prison, the one to which others hold the keys, the one to which others constrain you, is the precise negation of the prison to which each man, perhaps, aspires and which some, unconsciously or not, realize in their own lives.

In any event, Cres had gone off. Because once again he felt unjustly persecuted? Or simply because he wanted to continue his insane revenge and escape punishment? This, for Rogas, was the question. A question of conscience, however, not of technicalities. Technically, when Cres became a "wanted man," incriminating himself by his flight (for officially flight signifies guilt, despite Rogas's dissenting opinion), the investigative problem could be considered resolved: tomorrow or within a year, Cres would be captured or killed ("killed in an exchange of gunfire with the police"); or he would continue to flee and to elude his hunters, and at a certain point he might even die a natural death; yet even if hundreds of people, following his example, were to devote themselves to the sport of killing judges, all the murdered judges would be laid at his door, just as all rivers flow (or used to flow) into the sea.

From the police station, Rogas telephoned the district attorney in Algo, requesting a warrant to search the Cres house, the search to be carried out at night and in the absence of the owner. The district attorney, not informed of the course of the investigation, wished to know the whole story, but Rogas had only to mention the verdict rendered against Cres, attempted homicide, for his curiosity to fade to a "So we're dealing with a jailbird" and for him to promise the warrant. After which, having got directions to the General Carco Culture Club, where he knew he would be able at that hour to find one of Cres's oldest and most trusted friends, Rogas set out

33

for the club, allowing worries and frustrations to be dispelled in the contemplation of the doorways, balconies, and courtyards that followed one after another on the narrow, tortuous streets of that old quarter of the town. Upon entering the club, located in a charming little triangular square, one did not see what it might have to do with culture. For that matter, its being named after General Carco, to whom the world is indebted for the burning of the entire Palatine Library, would have been enough to put one on one's guard. Inside the club were two billiard tables and four card tables, a side table on which lay a hunting magazine and a newspaper, numerous chairs, and two consoles with mirrors that reflected the absorbed, almost funereal, groups of card and billiard players. The silence was broken only by the dry click of the balls on the flat, faded-green surfaces of the billiard tables, and by the more prolonged and, it would seem, more joyous sound of the balls that rolled into pockets. For a moment and almost imperceptibly, the entrance of Rogas distracted the players' attention. Rogas made a small bow, to which no one responded, and then he asked, "Dr. Maxia?" Without raising his eyes from his cards, one of the players said, "I am Dr. Maxia. What do you want?" "I want to talk to you," Rogas said. Brusquely, so as to allow him no illusion about being able to put off the conversation until after the end of the game. The tone of voice had its effect. "I will be with you at once," Maxia said. Delicately, he laid down the fan of cards, relinquished his place to a man who had been standing behind him, an attentive spectator of his game. He walked over to Rogas. "At your disposal," he said.

"Thank you. I am—"

"Let us go outside, if you don't mind," the Doctor interrupted. And no sooner outside: "You are Inspector Rogas. I've seen a photograph of you in a newspaper."

"Yes, I'm Rogas."

"And you're investigating this chain of crimes that —"

"Yes," Rogas admitted.

"But I don't see how I can be of any help to you." The smile ceremonious, the forehead creased with uneasiness.

"Please. Indeed, I must ask your pardon for having taken you away from your game. But it's a matter of a little verification, a check I must make. It concerns your friend Cres. Nothing directly related to the investigation I am working on, of course. It is simply a check to eliminate the coincidences, those apparent connections that turn up in the course of an investigation and that one must eliminate in order to move ahead."

"I understand," Maxia said, who did not understand.

"I have been told that you are the only person Cres frequents."

"That is not quite the case. He, to use your expression, does not frequent me. It is I who look him up, who try to draw him out of his shell, make him pick up old habits again, bring him in contact with other people. But it's a waste of time. Now and then I'm tempted to give up, particularly because it seems to me that I am annoying him with my attentions."

"Interesting," Rogas said.

"What?" Maxia asked, in a flush of suspicion.

"What you say."

"But, excuse me, what exactly do you want to know?"

35

"Nothing exactly. I just want you to talk to me about Cres, about his personality, how he lives."

"I'd rather you ask me questions. Talking like that, freely, I'm afraid I may say something that someone who doesn't know him can misconstrue, something that, if picked up by you, can even turn out to harm him."

"Don't be afraid of that. Nothing you tell me will appear in any memorandum, any report. Our talk is confidential. I want to get an idea of the man, of the personality."

"A strange personality," Maxia said.

"Look, I'll ask you a specific question. In your opinion, was he innocent?"

"I want to be frank. For a while, I believed he really had tried to put his wife out of the way. He's always been a closed sort, taciturn, morose; you can believe anything, good or bad, of a man like that. Just try to understand what goes on in the head of a man like that. So, an indictment comes along, based on circumstantial evidence but in theory credible; the indictment is followed by a verdict of guilty; the verdict is upheld on appeal. . . . A person believes that. I believed it."

"Guilty."

"Yes, guilty . . . Then his wife begins to behave in a kind of way . . . as if she were satisfied, gratified, happy —a happiness she'd like to hide but which bursts out in every gesture, every word. . . ."

"Nothing more?"

"Nothing more. And then, as you know, she disappeared."

"She could be dead. Killed, I mean."

"Why? By whom? Where? . . . Her husband was in jail.

And no one else could have any reason to take revenge on a wife who, unjustly or justly, had had her husband thrown into prison for five years."

"It could have been a hired killer."

"I rule that out. Without passing any judgment on whether or not Cres would be capable of hiring a killer. I rule it out for the simple fact that the very day before she disappeared, his wife had completed transactions to convert everything she owned into cash."

"Right," Rogas said approvingly. "Now tell me, did Cres know while he was in prison that his wife had disappeared?"

"I believe so."

"You don't know?"

"No, I don't know. Never once, from the day he got out of jail, has he said one word about his wife."

"Not even about the machinations he was the victim of, not about the unfair verdict?"

"Not even that. Never."

"What does Cres talk about? When he's with you, I mean. There surely must be some topic that turns up frequently in your conversation. . . . An interest, a preference . . . Books, politics, sports, women, crime news . . ."

"Let's see. . . . But, if I'm not mistaken, a moment ago you said 'unfair verdict.' Did you say that to pretend you're on my side, or are you really convinced that Cres was convicted unfairly?"

"Not entirely. Seventy percent, let's say. . . . So what does he talk about when he is with you?"

"He doesn't talk about women. You know, that wouldn't be talking about a rope in a hanged man's house; that would be the hanged man himself talking about a rope. . . . He doesn't know anything about sports, doesn't care about politics, doesn't read many books. . . . I'd say he likes to talk about human-interest stories —the most obscure, complicated kind, full of double meanings. . . . But with detachment, with a light touch— with relish, the way a person would talk who enjoys an absurd spectacle, a hoax. . . . Come to think of it, like someone who's been the victim of a hoax and now is amused to see other people fall into the same trap."

"Amused?"

"Maybe he's pretending to be amused. . . . The Reis trial, for example. He's followed the news reports on it in three or four papers, talked about it often."

"Ah, the Reis case!"

"Don't misunderstand me, please. Cres doesn't side with the defendant. He isn't convinced the man's innocent, nor does he find any justification for the crime he's accused of."

"And when they killed District Attorney Varga?"

"Nothing."

"But he did talk about it?"

"Yes, but only from what you might call a technical angle. Since the District Attorney was dead, would there be a new trial or would the law allow for a substitute—"

"And Cres hoped for a substitute, not for a new trial."

"How do you know that?"

"I'm guessing."

Maxia's expression became diffident, perplexed. He was beginning to wonder whether he had said too much, whether he should watch his tongue. Rogas sensed that

38

the moment had come to change the subject. "Cres isn't here," he said.

"He's not where? At home? In town?"

"He's not at home or in town. Disappeared."

"What do you mean, disappeared? How can you be sure he's not at home?"

"I went to his house, I knocked again and again. Not a sound."

"He's pretending not to be home. With me, too, sometimes. But I ignore it, I don't get offended. He doesn't like to be with people, sometimes not even with me. . . . Once, I read the diary of a sixteenth-century Florentine painter—pretty squalid stuff, a neurotic's story. But I was reminded of it precisely in connection with Cres. Because the painter used to hear his friends knock and call out to him, and he would pretend not to be at home; then he would write in his diary, 'So-and-So and So-and-So knocked; I don't know what they wanted,' and he would think about it for two whole days. . . ."

"Pontormo," Rogas said.

"That's right, Pontormo. . . . How did you know?"

"I'm guessing," Rogas said, ironically this time.

"Pontormo," Maxia repeated, disconcerted. "Well, when I'm standing outside Cres's door, sure that he's there and doesn't want to open, I take the edge off the irritation that grips me for a second by thinking of Pontormo, and how Cres is letting me stand there for the pleasure of wasting two days daydreaming about what I might have wanted—when he knows perfectly well I don't want a thing—and feeling remorseful for having treated me badly."

"Pontormo comes through in his diary as a hypochondriac. What would you say to that?"

"I'd agree."

"Cres, too, then."

"Since I'm a doctor, with regard to Cres I'd be more cautious."

"Right. But this time, my dear Doctor, I believe that Cres really isn't at home, that he's gone away. . . . Now, tell me this: are you sure he was at home all those times you found yourself waiting in front of his door?"

"What do you mean, sure? I've no proof. Nor can I say always. It's possible that sometimes he actually wasn't there."

"But you have always suspected that he was."

"The first times, no. Then, after checking with the neighbors, who said they hadn't seen him go out, I came to that conclusion. And for that matter, it fits the type of person he is, as far as I know him."

"Has it happened recently that you've been left standing more often than usual in front of a closed door?"

"I don't remember. . . . It's happened to me often enough, yes, but I can't say whether it's been more often than last year or three years ago."

"I want to tell you, in all candor, that we are looking for Cres to question him in connection with this massacre of judges. In the last few days, we've had him under surveillance, and up until yesterday evening, according to the police, he's been at home. Now, I have the clear impression that he's no longer there, that he's managed to elude the stakeout and make a getaway. I've asked the district attorney for a search warrant. Tonight, if Cres is not there, as I assume, or if he pretends not to be there,

40

as you believe, we will force the door and search the house. In the circumstances, I hope you, as a friend of Cres and in his interest, will be willing to accompany me."

"I'll come. But first I'd like us to go together now and try to get him to answer the door."

"That's fine with me," Rogas said.

Cres was not there. Rogas observed with what order and neatness the house, too large for a man living alone, was kept. But something sinister hovered in the air, as in prisons or convents. A more concretely sinister detail, it seemed to Rogas, was a portrait of Mrs. Cres (languid glance, lips half-parted as if she were about to pronounce a word of love) that looked out from a heavy silver frame: it was placed opposite the double bed in which, evidently, Cres had continued to sleep, since on top of the bed table there were ranged, in orderly fashion, water thermos and glass, bicarbonate of soda, cough lozenges, ashtray, and the third and last volume of *The Brothers Karamazov*. Under the book was one of those memorandum cards that come packaged with expensive cigarettes; the Inspector surmised that Cres had used it as a bookmark; if it was not inside the book, one could assume that he had come to the end: "Well, now we will finish talking and go to his funeral dinner. Don't be put out at our eating pancakes—it's a very old custom and there's something nice in that!" . . . Perhaps he had finished the book while waiting for it to be time for him to slip away, having set everything in order in anticipation of the police's breaking in during his absence. A precise, meticulous man, he had left nothing that could serve to

41

identify or trace him—not a photograph, not a hotel bill, not a railroad ticket stub, no receipt whatever. The identity of the man who until a few hours ago had inhabited the house was fading away into the few things that remained by the bed: the bicarbonate, the cough lozenges, the *Karamazov*. . . . Bicarbonate and lozenges were almost finished, and so he had left them behind; one could deduce that he consumed them in quantity, since he ate complicated things (in the kitchen were some of the more rare and highly spiced culinary ingredients) and smoked Turkish cigarettes. As for the *Karamazov,* one could account for that choice by virtue of the fact that in the meager collection on the bookshelves, the Russians up to Gorki were in the majority.

The empty portrait frames in the house sparked a sudden seizure of awareness in Maxia. He remembered very well one of the vanished photographs. It was of Cres standing and leaning slightly, in an attitude of affectionate concern, toward his seated mother; the old lady, holding an open fan in one hand, was all intent that the camera's eye should capture that gesture of abiding flirtatiousness. Why had Cres removed it? Obviously because he did not want a likeness of himself to fall into the hands of the police; this was confirmed by the fact that photographs of his mother, his father, his wife, and many strangers who must have been relatives or friends were found by the dozen in a large box, but not one of him, not even of his first Communion. Maxia's loyalty to his friend began to wane, the more so as that sleepless night began to weigh on him. For Rogas, however, the disappearance of the photographs presented itself as a problem within a problem: either Cres had removed them out of some kind of superstition, dictated by a neurotic fear about leaving his own likeness to fall into the hands of people who were not friendly toward him (for even in the nervous disorders of a reasonably cultivated man, the most primitive and unlikely superstitions may surface), or he had done so to prevent the police's using them to track him down by distributing them throughout the country and having them published in the papers. But in this case, the ploy was of little moment: within a few hours, Rogas would have—both from the office that issues passports and from the records of the prison where Cres had sojourned—the photographs necessary for the hunt that would be unleashed. Not to mention that also in newspaper and picture-agency files there must be some photographs from the time of the trial. Unless . . . And there flashed into his mind the recollection of what disorder and neglect reigned over things that were supposed to be preserved and cared for; how relatively easy it was to remove from historical archives a decree of Charles VI or a note of General Carco, and from court archives the bound copy of trial proceedings. Rogas had a presentiment that he would not find a photograph of Cres anywhere.

He did not, in fact, find any. Nor could he make use of the two published in newspapers ten years before: in one Inspector Contrera appeared in focus, and in the other the defense lawyer; in both, Cres was like a shape behind smoked glass. There was a famous police artist who had once succeeded in having a thief arrested by sketching his face from a description supplied by the robber's victim; in two days of work, with Dr. Maxia constantly offering descriptions and suggesting corrections, the artist eventually produced a portrait the distribution of which would have risked causing harassment to a celebrated film star.

What was circulated was the verbal description of a man five feet eight inches tall, thin, dark-skinned, slightly bald, with some white hair, perfect teeth, and slightly aquiline nose; by preference, the man wore gray; he had a great deal of money. This last was the factor that made him virtually invulnerable, provided that in his travels and stopovers he kept to first-class accommodations, which the police were reluctant to search.

Cres had become, in a word, invisible.

Rogas also suspected exactly how Cres had managed to get himself documents for a new identity. In prison, he had known one of the most able counterfeiters in the country, perhaps the best known to the police of four or five nations. The counterfeiter was a reliable man, scrupulous and loyal in regard to his clients. Fellow-prisoners, questioned in this respect, recalled that he was very close to Cres during their years in jail. Rogas went to visit him, for he, too, was now at liberty, but the man said that in prison he had played chess with Cres and talked about books, that he remembered him warmly, but that outside of prison he had not seen him again and, indeed, was eager to have news of him. Was he well? Had they reviewed his trial? If the Inspector had occasion to see him, would the Inspector be kind enough to give Cres his greetings? Rogas had not expected a different attitude.

At this point, Rogas's investigation had reached a fairly reliable presumptive solution. Now it was necessary to find Cres, and the first thing to be done was to check hotel registers in the cities where the crimes had been committed for the days when they had occurred, verifying whether from one city to the next, on the dates of the crimes, the same name might not turn up; that name would be the one Cres had taken for his false papers. Not that Rogas really hoped to get any positive results, but it was a job that had to be done. Furthermore, so many criminal cases he had worked on had taught him that no matter how perfect the plan, how carefully worked out the details, subtleties, and nuances, the most stupid, the most clumsily patched-up mistake always and unforeseeably slipped in to ruin its author.

But while the Inspector, having returned to the capital, was preparing a complete report on his work, District Attorney Perro was felled in the capital. This time there were witnesses: a night watchman, a prostitute, and a man who, because of the heat, was out on his balcony. None of the three had actually seen the crime committed, but immediately after hearing the shot, all three had seen two people running away. From the speed and agility of the culprits' flight, the witnesses could say positively that they were young; from their hair and style of dress (since, for a second, they had paused uncertainly under a street lamp), the witnesses could say further that they were young men of a certain type. "First the rebels revolutionized the style of wearing their hair . . . not molesting the mustache or beard, which they allowed to keep on growing as long as it would . . . letting it hang down in great length and disorder in the back. . . . [They] decided to wear the purple stripe on their togas. . . . And the sleeves of their tunics were cut tight above the wrists. . . . Their cloaks, trousers, and boots were also different:

and these, too, were called the Hun style, which they imitated." (Procopius of Caesarea, *Secret History.*)

The news cheered the entire, or almost the entire, nation. Uplifted were the morale and morals of Parliament, Administration, press, clergy, fathers of families, and academics. Also of the working class and of the International Revolutionary Party, which represented it. Not one paper spared the police veiled sarcasm or open derision. The question that reporters and commentators, members of the government and of the opposition, asked each other and asked in diverse ways was: How was it possible that, in a country agitated by insurrectional cadres that preached violence as both means and end, the police had opted for the thesis of the solitary criminal, the mad revenger?

The High Commissioner of Police and the Minister for National Security were asking themselves the same thing. Their questions descended on Rogas like an avalanche. In vain, the Inspector tried to make his chief understand how nothing that had occurred lessened the validity of the thesis pursued to that point, that the unanimous testimony of three well-deserving citizens must be considered within the limits of what actually had been seen; i.e., two young men running away from the scene of the crime. His chief took umbrage at this: he enjoined Rogas to get that Cres out of his head; poor man, perhaps he had run away because he was being unjustly persecuted; Rogas should set to work instead with his colleague in the Political Section, if he wished to redeem himself and redeem the police force from evident error.

Rogas did not get Cres out of his head; now, thanks to a night watchman, a prostitute, and a gentleman suffering from the heat, Cres could proceed with the execution of his plan, enjoying practically boundless freedom and immunity. Rogas's professional interest had ebbed; however, there remained his human concern and punctilio. He would meet Cres, one day or another—maybe not to arrest him, but if he had to do so, he would. Meanwhile, off to work under the orders of his colleague in the Political Section—punishment; in effect, demotion.

The offices of the Political Section looked like a newly established branch of a Benedictine library: at each table, an official immersed in reading a book, a leaflet, a magazine; everywhere piles of books, leaflets, and magazines with threatening or incomprehensible titles. "We're in the process of scanning all the publications the revolutionary cadres have put out over the last six months. We concentrate on articles or passages that attack the administration of justice in our country," his section-head colleague explained to him. "So far, we've found three or four that are more or less violent, but our favorite is this one." He picked up a magazine printed on heavy, pale-yellow paper, opened it, showed Rogas a page marked in the margin in red and densely underlined in blue. "Read that; it's one of those things deliberately designed to inflame weak minds, to unhinge people who have already lost their grip on reality."

Rogas read it absently. He was thinking about a grip on reality—his colleague's, Cres's. "Actually," he said, handing the magazine back, "it is a pretty strong article. Prosecutable, I'd say, for contempt; maybe also for inciting to crime."

47

"Already attended to, my dear colleague, already attended to." Condescending emphasis on the word "colleague," as if to convey that in fact they were no such thing. "But the problem is, who wrote it? Yes, of course, on the incrimination angle we've got the editor of the magazine. But the article is anonymous. Did he write it, did he not write it? . . . Because, you see, I've got an idea that the shots—these murders of judges, I mean—come from the cadre that publishes this magazine. Do you know how I got the idea? Because lately this group—we keep it under surveillance, of course—has sort of fallen apart. There are maybe ten people left for us to keep an eye on. Most of the cadre has disappeared, and we can't find them."

"You don't suppose it's the time of year that has scattered them?" Rogas was struck by the fact that the police were so mesmerized by the word "cadre" that they pronounced it as if it were within quotes. "They've gone off to the shore, to the mountains; they're traveling abroad. . . ."

"We've thought of that. Maybe they are at the shore or in the mountains. But in hiding."

"No, no. They're at their fathers' country houses or on their fathers' yachts. I'll bet the ones who've stayed behind under surveillance are the poorest ones."

"That may be." Letting the objection drop: "The editor of the magazine has disappeared, too. . . . Now, I would like you to fish him up for me—not to arrest or detain him, of course."

"It won't be easy."

"Easier for you than for us, I assume. You are almost a man of letters." This in a tone of voice that tried to be

48

ingratiating but that betrayed facetious scorn, for Rogas
had this bad reputation among his superiors and colleagues on account of the books he kept on his office
desk and the clarity, coherence, and succinctness of his
written reports. These were so unlike the ones that had
been circulating in police offices for at least a century
that they often sparked the shout "How this character
can write!" or again "What's this fellow trying to say?"
It was known, furthermore, that he frequented journal-
ists and authors. And he was said to go to art galleries
and to the theatre.

"I am not 'almost a man of letters,' " Rogas said
brusquely.

"I'm sorry. I meant to say, you are well acquainted
with those people."

"Not even that. I know three or four newsmen; very
few literary men, actually. And I've been a friend of the
writer Cusan from grammar-school days."

"In any event, you are in a better position to handle
this job than we are. . . . You will, first, find out where
the magazine editor is hiding and inform me immediately, so that I can set up a strict surveillance; second,
when the stakeout is functioning, you will pay the fellow
a visit, talk to him, pump him for all the information you
can get about the magazine and the cadre—scare him a
little so that he does something to scare his friends, too.
Needless to say, we'll tap the phone of the house where
he's hiding. . . . O.K.?"

"O.K.," Rogas said wearily.

The editor of the magazine *Permanent Revolution* was
the guest, as Rogas promptly learned, of the writer

Nocio. Rogas notified his colleague in the Political Section, who immediately arranged for house surveillance and a wiretap. Two hours later, he was knocking at the door of a small villa on the outskirts of the city, where Nocio habitually went each summer to write that summer's book.

A maid in apron and starched lace cap opened the door, examined him with distrust, and, before Rogas had uttered a word, said, "Mr. Nocio isn't in."

"I am a police inspector."

"I will see if he's in," the maid said, flushing either over the lie she had just proffered or from the emotion, never before experienced in that household, at finding herself confronted by a police inspector.

Nocio was in. The maid ushered Rogas into a large, dark study; at the far end, before a desk on which the light of a gooseneck lamp fell—and it was bright daylight outdoors—sat Nocio. When the Inspector was two steps away, he raised his eyes from the manuscript he appeared to be correcting; he rose, leaning on the arms of his chair as if with an effort, came around the desk, offered his hand.

"I am Inspector Rogas."

"Delighted. I am at your service." Spreading his hands wide, as much as to say that there was very little he, in his inveterate state of innocence, could do for the police who, everyone knows, are always looking for the guilty.

"I am disturbing you," Rogas said, "because it appears that Dr. Galano, the editor of the magazine *Permanent Revolution,* is your guest."

"Not mine. My wife's."

"Ah," said Rogas.

"Don't think what you're thinking," Nocio said, laughing. "My wife has passed the canonical age. The fact of the matter is, she acts as his housekeeper; she is housekeeper to a priest of the revolution. Furthermore, strictly between ourselves, Galano—"

"His personal tastes are known."

"Of course, you people know everything. . . . And so you knew"—ironically—"that Galano is my guest: a piece of information that is not entirely correct. He is the guest of my wife. Just between us, I can't stand him. He's a hysterical little provincial intellectual. What am I saying, intellectual! He's one of those cretins who create the illusion of intelligent discourse. It takes very little today to acquire that magical skill. 'Words, words, words . . .' You read his magazine?"

"Some articles. In line of duty."

Nocio fell into a chair, prey to almost silent but uncontainable, visceral laughter. " 'In line of duty!' Do you know, you've just made one of the most marvelous remarks I've heard in years? 'In line of duty.' Too utterly marvelous! . . . But please, do sit down." He gestured toward the chair opposite.

"Have you seen," Nocio continued, composing himself after his abrupt outburst of mirth, "the department in the magazine that deals with books? It's a column called 'The Index.' This cretin—Galano, I mean—has discovered the Index Librorum Prohibitorum. Four hundred and some years after the fact, when the Catholic Church itself is revoking it! . . . My books, all of them, systematically get put on his 'Index.' Think of it: *my* books! The most revolutionary books that have been written in these parts in the last thirty years."

51

Simple-minded, Rogas thought. He's come straight to the sore point. "That's right," he agreed aloud. But only by way of consolation.

"The fact is," Nocio went on, "they're all Catholics. Old-style, fanatical, funereal Catholics, and they don't know it. What a pity the Church is in such a hurry to bring itself up to date. If it were to retreat behind its old lines of defense, if it were to go back to being closed and cruel the way it used to be in the days of Philip II, the Inquisition, the Counter Reformation, these people would be joining up in droves. Prohibit, investigate, punish—that's what they want."

"But if that were to happen, the Church would bear down hard on us again, the way it did during the Counter Reformation. And you certainly don't want that," Rogas observed.

"No, I don't want it. And anyhow it can't happen. But I've got this crazy wish that it would; it's a dream of mine. Everything would be clearer, tidier: they on one side, me on the other. Instead, the way things are, I'm forced to be on their side, on the side of Galano, who puts me on his 'Index.' The revolution, you understand? This word, and it's only a word, involves me, blackmails me, binds me to Galano and his ilk." Almost a shout: "I hate him!"

A pause. Then Nocio stood up, went to the desk, picked up some sheets of paper; he came back and sat down in front of Rogas. "Do you know what I was doing when you came in? I was rereading and correcting a poem I ripped off—like that, in a rage—last evening. Poetry! I haven't written poetry since I was in high school. . . . Read it." He thrust the papers into Rogas's

hand with a nervous gesture, as if he had made a decision
he was ashamed of. Rogas read.

> Arrogant, you repeat from memory
> what you do not know,
> idea-spray, scum of old and new ideas
> (more old than new)
> that your mouths
> drool and dribble
> the way only yesterday
> in Mama's arms
> —Mama, Mama—
> they slobbered ice cream.
> And flowing from
> your beards of protomartyrs—
> that faddist fakery,
> fiction of a maturity
> that makes you
> equal to your fathers
> and therefore fit for incest.
> Mama . . .
> The whole problem right here,
> the woman who lies in your father's bed,
> and you announce her reign;
> and behind your beards you have faces
> like the San Luigi of a neo-neo-capitalism—
> all the flaws of the Gonzagas in his thin face,
> all the flaws of the middle class in your own;
> he grown up among dwarfs and buffoons,
> among hunchbacks and eunuchs;
> distilled by the pox,
> a saint because never did he look his mother,
> who was a woman,

53

in the face;
but yours you look in the face and think
she is a whore if she lies in the bed of your father
because you are holier than he
even if you do not know it,
and you have grown up—you, too—
among buffoons, dwarfs, and eunuchs,
between the gold and the lues;
the beard, then, to make sinister
the delicate faces of pimps
inverts
perverts;
and Robespierre, who had no beard,
laughs at you, at your revolution;
his skull laughs,
his dust,
his last particle of dust that is worth more
than your whole life—
that is, than the fact that you are alive while he is dead;
and Marx, too, who had a beard, laughs,
laughs with every bristle of his beard,
laughs at the empty husks he has left you,
the necklaces of jingling bells
of dry sperm, dead sperm
that you bedeck yourselves with like show mules;
you shake them in idleness, in discontent, in disgust
(the living seed of Marx is in those who suffer,
who think,
who have no flags).
Robespierre and Marx are laughing,
but perhaps they also weep
over the man, no longer human, who is fleshed in you,
over mind that does not think,
over heart that does not love,

54

over the perpetual fiasco of sex and mind
with which you announce the reign of the mothers.
"That is not what I meant at all;
that is not it, at all—"
Not that, not that,
not even we wanted that,
we buffoons
vitiated
corrupted;
we fathers,
not even we,
since we prostituted life but understood love,
prostituted mind but understood thought,
reason
sex
man and woman
male and female
grief
death.
Talleyrand said that the sweetness of life
was known only to those who, like him,
had lived before the Revolution,
but after you (not your revolution,
for you will not make one) there will no longer be
relic reflection echo
of the sweetness of life,
nor of you will there remain any record
unless it be
in the files of the federal narcotics bureau.
The human man has had his moon,
the human goddess
quiet light of love;
you have your
gray pumice pox-infected desert

deserving of your no longer human bones,
dead nature with the dead lights of judgment;
but you know nothing
of the Ariostoan fable of Orlando
restored to his senses by Astolfo
on a lunar voyage
of the mind sealed in a flask
like yours (but yours is
irrecuperable). The flask, still life,
the flask of Eros,
as Stendhal said in Italian in the text,
Stendhal whom you do not know,
Stendhal who speaks
the language of passion to which you are all dead.

"Interesting," Rogas said. "Will you publish it?"

"You must be joking." The delicate, thoughtful lines of his face changed and coarsened. A merchant, Rogas thought, who feels he's making a bid that will ruin him. "You must be joking. They're already pointing their fingers at me as a reactionary. If I bring out a thing like this, I'm done for. It would be my gravestone, my epitaph."

"But you had the impulse to write it; you've written it."

"I blew up, I blew up. It's of no importance. Crazy. You'll tell me there are some truths, some insights in it. But they don't count, not in comparison to the great, unique fact of the revolution. Which will come, which will come as surely as day follows night. . . . Oh, no, Galano won't make the revolution; people like him won't. . . . But it will come. And Galano and the rest who talk about it without understanding it and without really expecting it—they're all in there, in the front line. . . .

Maybe they'll be the first to be devoured, but meanwhile there they are, and there they will be until the moment it explodes." Changing his tone of voice: "You've read Pascal?"

"I've read him."

"You remember his idea about the wager? At first glance, it seems scandalous—"

"Monstrous, I'd say."

"It isn't. . . . If I believe in God, in eternal life, in the immortality of the soul—even if these things don't exist —what price must I pay? Nothing. But if I don't believe, and if these things do exist, the price to be paid is everlasting death. . . . Today the possibility of making the wager has shifted from metaphysics to history. Now the 'beyond' is the revolution. I would risk losing everything were I to bet against the revolution. But if I bet on it, I lose nothing if it doesn't take place; I win everything if it does. . . . And this is not, as you say, a monstrous proposition. Its utilitarian formulation mustn't make us forget that we are still caught up in the problem of what Augustine and Pascal called free choice, what I call liberty. . . . You don't have this problem? You don't bet? You don't like to bet?"

"I detest every kind of betting. I don't want to risk winning. And I've a soft spot for losing, for losers. I can tell you, too, that I'm discovering in myself a kind of affection for the revolution—precisely because it is already defeated."

"I would say, and I haven't the slightest wish to offend you, that that is a professional point of view. Because you are a part of the structure of the bourgeois state, in order to defend it you've come to the point of believing it has a practically inexhaustible survival potential. But don't you see what's happening in our country? Sooner or later, we must pay for our mistakes."

"When there is something to pay with," Rogas said morosely.

"Right, when there's something to pay with." He scrutinized Rogas with absent-minded attention. Then, jokingly: "Isn't talking about revolution a punishable offense?"

"Professionally, this time, I assure you that the more one talks about it, the better."

"O Galano!" he apostrophized comically. And suddenly he remembered why Rogas was there. "But you came to talk to Galano! Forgive me, I'll have him called at once." He went to the desk, took up a little silver bell, and rang it loudly. At the sound, the maid came. "Tell Mr. Galano—and, naturally, my wife, too—that a police inspector is here who wants to talk to him." The maid had no sooner disappeared than Nocio hastily gathered up the pages he had had Rogas read, put them in a drawer of the desk, locked the drawer, and pocketed the key.

"You'll destroy the poem?" Rogas asked.

"Why?" Surprised, irritated.

"You can't leave anything lying around that may make you lose your bet. . . . But I wonder—what if you could win the bet with the poem?"

"For the love of heaven!" Nocio said. Perhaps referring to the momentary folly of those verses, perhaps warning Rogas not to speak of them further, for Galano had entered the room in a kind of soundless balletic flight. He halted his dance before Nocio; feigning anxiety, consternation, he asked, "A police inspector? For me?"

Nocio indicated Rogas, who had risen to his feet.

"Are you going to arrest me?" Galano asked, languidly peering up at Rogas. He turned to Nocio. "Do you think he's come to arrest me?"

"I don't know," Nocio said brusquely.

"But you'd like that," Galano said, shaking his finger like someone who's caught another out and is scolding him.

"What is it he would like?" Mrs. Nocio asked from the door, in an I'll-fix-you tone of voice. Rogas bowed slightly. He thought, Tallemant des Réaux would say that few women are less lovely than she.

"For them to arrest me," Galano said.

"Oh," the woman murmured, looking with horror at her husband.

Fearing a small explosion of domestic resentments, Rogas said, "I must disappoint you. I haven't come to arrest you."

"You disappoint me indeed," Galano said. "And you disappoint him." Pointing to Nocio.

"I have come," Rogas said, "to inform you that, as editor of the magazine *Permanent Revolution* and, presumably, author of an unsigned article on the administration of justice, you have been accused of contempt and of inciting an act against the security of the state."

"The same old story," Galano said.

"Yes, the same old story. But this time in a different climate, you understand."

"No, I don't understand. Rather, I refuse to understand. Because if they want to make me the scapegoat for

59

that carrousel of murdered judges, it means that the administration of justice goes beyond our denunciations of it, so I will have material to write even more violent pieces about it."

"Then you did write the article?"

"I don't deny it and I don't admit it. You have informed me of the charges; we'll see each other in court. But I assure you, I am not someone who goes around killing judges."

"I am sure of that."

"Personally, or is it the police who are sure of it?"

"Personally."

"Why?" With a touch of disappointment.

"Perhaps out of pride in my work."

"Of course, I remember. You were on another scent. . . . But the police, instead, have some suspicions about me."

"I haven't said that. The police—this I can tell you— have some suspicions about your article; that is, about the effects an article like yours can produce on a reader who is *non compos mentis,* or on a group of readers, on an extreme group of your aficionados."

"Oh, no, my articles don't produce such effects, worse luck. If they did, he"—he pointed at Nocio—"would long since have been installed in the pantheon of Christ's Church, at rest among the nation's heroic dead."

Nocio's chin shook, like that of a child about to cry. But perhaps it was anger. "You are a swine," he said. And he tried to sweeten the insult by smiling as if it were a joke.

"Why, please? Because I maintain that you are a middle-class writer who has far more to answer for than the

Minister for Security or the President of the Supreme Court or the most abominable American financier?"

"I? A middle-class writer?" Turning to Rogas: "Did you hear? Now I am a middle-class writer! You tell him whether the police consider me a middle-class writer."

"Vilfredo, don't be ridiculous," his wife intervened. "Do you really need a certificate from the police: 'Vilfredo Nocio is not a middle-class writer.' Signed Tamborra?" (Tamborra was the High Commissioner of Police, known for his perfervid aversion to intellectuals.)

"Shut your mouth," Nocio said.

"There's instant proof of how reactionary you are: 'Shut your mouth.' Because I'm a woman, because I'm your wife—"

"You don't even have a mouth; you've got a beak, a parrot's beak, a magpie's beak," Nocio said ferociously.

"Oh, no, there's no help for it," Galano said. "You are a middle-class writer; you yourself are middle-class, you live like a middle-class man; you eat, sleep, and amuse yourself like a middle-class man—"

"I am *not* middle-class!" Nocio shouted. He was on the verge of breaking down.

"Excuse me," Rogas said to Galano, and his question was also a sympathetic attempt to ease Nocio's anguish. "You say, 'You live like a middle-class man; you eat, sleep, and amuse yourself like a middle-class man.' Precisely what do you mean?"

"You don't understand?"

"No, I don't understand."

"Why, all this . . ." Galano said. He raised his arms to encompass and circumscribe all that was implicit in the

61

study, the house, the encircling garden, and the life that Nocio led in those surroundings.

"Meanwhile you are staying here. And your own house is not all that different," Nocio said.

"But I am staying here with a difference, that's the point," Galano shrilled triumphantly.

"You eat the way I do; blue-collar people working for a wage serve you the way they serve me; you sleep in a canopied bed like mine. . . . In fact, in your own house you sleep in a bed they sold you, fobbed off on you as the Marquise de Pompadour's. . . ."

Galano bristled. "They did not fob it off on me. It's authentic. But that desk of yours, it doesn't come from D'Annunzio's villa at Arachon; it was manufactured a couple of years ago in Évian." He turned to Rogas. "Very significant, don't you think? He bought a desk because they made him believe D'Annunzio used to sit at it reading Petrarch."

"All right, my desk is a copy, your bed is genuine. The point is, you bought it and you sleep in it. . . . In a word, you live like me, spend your money like me, have the same friends and acquaintances I have. You do nothing but come and go between Saint-Moritz and Taormina and Monte Carlo. You gamble and you pay for your love affairs, which I don't do, which I have never done. But I am middle-class and you are not."

"To be or not to be middle-class depends on this," Galano said, and with his index finger he tapped the center of his forehead.

"Very convenient," Rogas said. He arose to leave.

"You wouldn't understand," Galano said scornfully.

The Chief of the Political Section was disappointed and tired. "No sooner had you left Galano," he related to Rogas, "than he got on the phone. He called, in this order, the director-general of the West Bank; the president of Schiele Pharmaceuticals; the editor of the government paper *Order and Freedom;* the editor of the opposition's weekly, the *Evening Red;* that famous tailor, Gradivo; the actress Marion Delavigue; the Count of Santo Spirito; and the ex-Queen of Moldavia. . . . *Merry Widow* stuff, isn't it? He informed all these people, with screams of laughter, that he had had a visit from a police inspector and it seemed the police suspected him of being the perpetrator of this systematic picking off of judges. Everyone was greatly amused. Now, do you believe people like that can be part of a revolutionary plot —what's more, that they can approve of actions like killing judges?"

"What about you?" He thought, In another minute, he'll be saddling me with responsibility for the idiotic idea of going after Galano.

"Not in my wildest dreams . . . All the same, from Galano's telephone calls we've come up with one useful little detail. At one point, when he was talking with the actress, he said that, if anything, the police should be looking into the people in Zeta. Zeta's the neo-anarchist group that's headed up by that ex-priest; he's a theorist in Christian evangelical anarchism. The group's financed by Narco, who is practically sole owner of the big SD store chain. SD—you know—it stands for Square Deal. I must say, it strikes me as a little much that evangelical neo-anarchists would be devoting themselves to an open

63

season on judges. But I will have to read the Bible, also all the publications these Zeta people put out."

"As far as the Bible is concerned, I can tell you unqualifiedly that you will find a great many injunctions against judging others and against judges. There is nothing evangelical, of course, about resorting to violence—slugging it out, as we policemen say. However, one doesn't know how priests and ex-priests read the Bible, when they read it. And then there's 'I came not to send peace, but the sword.'"

"Who says that?"

"Christ said it."

"Right, there is some talk about a sword. Still, I would never have thought that Christ—"

"It could be a metaphor. The sword, I mean."

"But a .38-caliber gun isn't. And *that*'s what we're dealing with. . . . That's why I don't trust the clue Galano's been kind enough to hand us."

"Nor do I."

"But we've got it, and we can't not look into it. . . . I think you're the person who should look into it. . . . Galano, while he was still talking to the actress, said, 'This evening, everybody's going to be at Narco's. If only the police knew . . .'"

"In my opinion, Galano suspected that the telephone was tapped and wanted to play a joke on us."

"You think so? . . . Well, joke or no joke, this evening you'll go to the Narco home. The house, naturally, will be surrounded—but discreetly—by plainclothesmen who will arrive a few at a time."

"Why don't you come along?"

"I can't. I've been called to see the Minister."

"Well, then, tell me what I must do, what I must say."

"Say that you want to have a talk with the ex-priest— I don't remember what the devil his name is—or that you're looking for such-and-such a person who you've been told is at the Narco home—invent any old name. . . . This notion, to be looking for someone who doesn't exist, strikes me as extremely good. . . . Anyhow, I trust your judgment, your discretion."

As Rogas, accompanied by a brigadier, was entering the baroque palace built by a cardinal and now occupied by Narco, the President of the Tribunal in Tera was shot dead. At that moment, however, the Inspector was not thinking of the crimes, or of Cres, who in all likelihood was their author; he was worried that he himself was slipping into a ridiculous position, and that his colleague in the Political Section would turn a cold shoulder to him once he hit rock bottom—rock bottom of the ridiculous, as well as of the erroneous.

He stated his name and rank to the doorman. Pressing a button, the man shouted that name, that rank into an invisible microphone. An authoritative voice was heard: "Have him come up. Servants' entrance." With a gesture of indolent scorn, the doorman pointed out the servants' stairway to Rogas.

The door was open, and the major-domo was standing there as if to bar their passage. "What is it you want?"

"To speak with Mr. Narco."

"I don't know if he can receive you now."

"Go ask him."

The man came back with an expression in which arrogance was diluted with amusement. Rogas felt a certain

65

foreboding: the faces of servants always foretell the mood of the masters. A long hallway, a deliciously furnished sitting room, a salon with many paintings. Watteau, Fragonard, Boucher. May they at least be fakes, Rogas hoped. Still another door, and they were in a great drawing room crowded with people. Instantly, Rogas knew that his colleague in the Political Section had lied to him: he had not been summoned by the Minister if that same Minister was now walking toward him together with a man who must be Narco.

With a grave face and in a menacing tone of voice, the Minister asked, "What do you want?"

Rogas elected not to recognize him. "To speak with Mr. Narco," he said quietly.

"I am he," the other man said. The Minister made him a sign that signified: You be quiet. It's up to me to put these boors in their place. He turned to Rogas: "Who are you?"

"I am Inspector Rogas. And you?"

"He's asking me who I am," the Minister said to Narco, smiling with irony and spite.

"Yes, he's asking you who you are," Narco shot back. Doubly pleased: both at the Minister's wounded vanity and at the painful situation in which the Inspector would shortly find himself.

"You really do not recognize me?"

"*I* do," the brigadier said, as exultant as the boy who answers the question his classmate has been unable to answer. Rogas was a good actor; he looked at the brigadier with surprise and vexation. Almost in a whisper, the brigadier said to him, "It's our Minister."

That "our" placated the Minister. He looked at Rogas

with the expression of a man who is disposed to be merciful but is waiting to be asked. Rogas said, "I beg your pardon, Excellency, but I did not expect—"

"You did not expect what? To find me here, at the home of my friend Narco?"

"I meant to say, I didn't expect to intrude on an evening among friends."

"You have intruded. So?"

"We came to ask Mr. Narco just one bit of information: whether he knows a man by the name of Zervo."

"Why should I know him?" Narco asked.

"Because they have told us that he belongs to the Neo-Anarchic Christian Movement, or that he frequents the group without belonging."

"I've never heard that name," Narco said. "But let's see if some of our friends know him. . . . Come along." All four moved toward the circle of people, seated or standing, who had drawn closer together to whisper and snicker the moment Rogas and the brigadier had entered. Moving into the circle, Rogas noticed Galano elegantly curled up in a big armchair. And that was no surprise.

"My dear Inspector," Galano greeted him cheerfully. Turning to the Minister, "I must say to you, my dearest Evaristo, you are one big liar. You've always denied that the police tap our telephones, but they do tap them, and how! The presence of the Inspector here is absolute proof of it."

Evaristo turned pale. He asked Rogas, "Is this true?"

Rogas said, "I've heard nothing about it."

"How delicious!" Galano said. "This one asks whether it is true, the other one says it isn't. . . ." He stood up to

67

confront the Minister. "Do you think I'm an imbecile? Don't hesitate, tell me: 'You are an imbecile, and I expect you to believe what I say and what the Inspector says.' "

"I give you my word, I know nothing about any wiretaps. . . . I can't exclude the possibility that sometimes they are made, but always on a court order and in the case of people under serious suspicion. . . . But political wiretaps, no. I rule that out absolutely."

"Well, then, I am a person under serious suspicion, because certainly my phone is tapped. . . . Not mine, to be exact: the phone of Vilfredo Nocio."

A salvo of outraged surprise arose from the bystanders.

"However that may be," Galano continued, "I want to give you some advice. Instead of playing out the farce with your Inspector, call him to the Ministry and have him tell you how and why he came here this evening."

"Be at my office tomorrow at ten," the Minister said to Rogas.

"Naturally," Galano said, "I won't know what you'll say to each other tomorrow. But I do know what I know. And I'm sorry, but in the next number of the *Permanent Revolution* you'll see—"

"Let it go," Narco said.

"Oh, no, I can't let him get away with this."

"Meantime, let's have a drink," Narco said. And he shouted to the waiter, "Bring the Inspector a drink."

Rogas remembered the phrase "but meanwhile bring the father something to drink" in a famous, tedious Italian novel, and thought how well the episode of that earlier trying visit matched the present moment. But he said to himself, "You're becoming paranoid; you're not Fra Cristoforo."

"Scotch, Armagnac, champagne?" Narco asked.

"No, thank you."

"Have a drink," the Minister said. "You're not on duty. The assignment you came here on is over and done with."

The next day at ten, in the Minister's anteroom, Rogas found the Chief of the Political Section. He, too, had been summoned, and on barely a half hour's notice; he was, therefore, breathless, upset, terrified, and Rogas's calm heightened his terror, in his certainty that such calm on Rogas's part came from the latter's decision to unload on him all responsibility for the unfortunate expedition to the Narco home. It would have been fair for him, in the Minister's presence, to assume the responsibility, but instead he was frantically wondering how he might attribute to Rogas defects in the execution of the plan, if not the idea for it.

But the Minister's mood, jovial and just short of hail-fellow-well-met, dissolved the terrors of the Chief of the Political Section proportionately as, on the other hand, it troubled Rogas.

After a cordial, vigorous handshake, the Minister sought to underscore the friendly nature of the meeting by moving from his cold and gleaming desk, crowded with telephones and push buttons, over to a corner of the big room which, thanks to armchairs, a small table, and a tiny bar, seemed family-like and intimate. To get the conversation started and, even more, to remove a thorn that was hurting him, he asked Rogas, smiling, "Tell me, did you really not recognize me yesterday evening?"

"I recognized you immediately, Your Excellency, but I wanted to play for time, to find out just what the situation—"

"Good," the Minister said. And turning to the Chief of the Political Section: "No point in telling you that last night's business was a mistake on your part, but—"

"Your Excellency, I—"

"—but, as I was saying, I never cry or lose my temper over spilt milk. Also, mistakes sometimes produce results that, even if they're not what one wanted, turn out to be useful beyond one's hopes. Last evening's blunder in the Narco drawing room produced, as its first effect, a victory for Galano, who had contrived to play a trick on the police and to get proof of wiretaps. . . . It embarrassed me, too, of course. . . . But then, after I'd left, it occurred to me, as I was thinking about the conduct of the police and the coincidence of my being at Narco's that very evening—I hadn't been there for two weeks—that the whole thing could be construed quite differently. That is, that neither I nor the police are fools, and, on our side, there must be a trap into which Galano, thinking he'd trapped us, had fallen. Devilishly sensitive, these people, full of fantasies. . . . By dint of turning themselves inside out to guess what our scheme was—we, unfortunately, weren't able even to think one up—within the space of two hours they had slipped from sarcastic self-confidence into abject terror. Galano, during the night, moved from Nocio's house to Schiele's: he was afraid of being arrested. And there were a lot of other transfers—from one host to another, from the person's own house to the house of a friend."

"Crazy," Rogas said.

"Crazy," the Minister said. "But, my dear Inspector, I am playing precisely on these crazy reactions of theirs. I stand in the middle; I offer protection one moment, a threat the next. The more they believe in the threat, the higher the price I put on protection. Because groups like those of Galano and Narco—and especially Narco's, those Catholic revolutionaries—are a convenience for me. They're almost as great a convenience for me as the Square Deal chain, which, as you know, is Narco's thing. To put it crudely, I deal (and that's the word that fits the case) in today's egg and tomorrow's chicken by being with them. The egg of power and the chicken of revolution. . . . You know what the political situation is—the, so to speak, structured political situation. One can sum it up in two words: it has suddenly dawned on my party, which has been misgoverning for thirty years, that it would misgovern better in collaboration with the International Revolutionary Party; and especially if that chair"—he gestured toward his own, behind the desk—"were to be occupied by the I.R.P's Secretary-General, Mr. Amar. Now, the vision of Mr. Amar sitting in that chair and ordering out the troops to fire on striking workers, or on farmers asking for water or students asking not to study—like my late predecessor, but even going him one better—this vision, I must confess, beguiles me, too. But today being today, it's a dream. Mr. Amar is no fool. He knows very well that it's better for me to sit in that chair than for him, better for me to sit

71

there in the sense that so long as I am there everybody is better off, Mr. Amar included."

"Under the leadership of Your Excellency, this Ministry—" the Chief of the Political Section began unctuously.

"It's trumpery, I know. I also know that you'd prefer to take orders from Mr. Amar, but you'll just have to be patient—"

"Your Excellency!" protested the Chief of the Political Section.

"Come, come—I know and I don't mind at all. As I told you, I'd hand over my post to Mr. Amar willingly. But, you see, this country hasn't reached the point yet of despising Mr. Amar's party as much as it despises mine. And in our system, contempt is what puts the seal of approval on power. Mr. Amar's people are doing their level best to deserve it, and with time they will. And once they've got it, they will know what to do to legitimize it. Because, while the system allows us to come to power via contempt, it is iniquity, the practice of iniquity, that legitimizes it. We—those of us in my party who succeed each other in ministerial posts—we are blandly iniquitous. Constitutionally and contingently iniquitous because we do not know how, we are unable, to be more iniquitous. On the contrary, we grow increasingly less so. But you people thirst after iniquity. Not only you, the police, I mean."

The Chief of the Political Section was looking at the Minister with the eyes of a hare caught in the beam of a headlamp. The Minister was looking sardonically at him. Rogas, too, who was thinking about the Minister. No cretin, he—even if he had the impression that the man was reciting things he had heard others say.

"To cheer you up," the Minister said to the Chief of the Political Section, "and also to make you realize what credits you are accumulating—you'll be able to turn them to good account someday—let me tell you that what you are doing, what I am having you do, corresponds fully to the wishes of Mr. Amar."

"What am I doing, Your Excellency?"

"You don't know?" the Minister said, with ironic amazement. "Well, just keep it up, all of you keep it up. . . . Bedeviling the cadres, as much as you can. Searches, distraints, arrests—always, naturally, with the authorization of the courts. . . . Another judge was murdered last evening, so they'll give you everything you want."

"Your Excellency," Rogas said," it seems to me we have gone off the right track to follow a wrong one. In connection with the murders of the judges, I mean."

The Minister looked at Rogas with sympathy and suspicion. He said, "Perhaps. But, right track or wrong, stay on it, stay on it."

Leaving the Ministry, "What do you make of that?" the Chief of the Political Section asked Rogas.

"I have no opinions. If I did, I'd change jobs. I've only got principles. What about you?"

"I've got neither opinions nor principles. But this talk of the Minister's—"

"I saw. You were upset by it."

"No, it didn't upset me. It takes something else to do that."

"What, then?"

"Nothing . . . I was just thinking. Why is he telling me —us—these things?"

"Right, us."

"There has to be some reason, some purpose."

"I am sure you will discover it," Rogas said, veiling sarcasm with flattery.

"Of course." Swallowing the flattery.

"Meanwhile what do we do?"

"What do we do?" the other man echoed.

"With your permission, I'd like to call on the President of the Supreme Court. Sooner or later, it will be his turn."

"What?"

"To be murdered. Whether it's my man who does it, or your cadres."

"You believe they'd dare go as far as the President of the Supreme Court?"

"Why not?"

"My god!" It was almost a groan.

"I'd say one should warn him."

"Of course. But with care, with tact."

"Do you want to go?" It was the right way to make the Chief of the Political Section feel reconfirmed in his authority and fearful of the responsibility.

"No, no, you go. I have too much else to do." That is, nothing.

"All right, I'll go this afternoon."

The President of the Supreme Court lived on the top floor of a small mansion buried in a green park just outside the city walls. It had once been the summer resi-

74

dence of the Dukes of San Concordio. The Society for the Protection of Forests and Woodlands had made a fuss over the park's being turned into a residential area, but now in that area there resided two or three members of the Society's board of governors, as well as a pair of Ministers, a dozen Deputies (of diverse political allegiances), as well as the Attorney General and the President of the Supreme Court.

One entered this residential enclave through well-guarded gates. Rogas got in by showing the porter his identification card and with the endorsement of a police agent stationed beside the glass-and-concrete booth in which the porter was caged. The small avenue that led to the building where President Riches lived was pointed out to him. It unfolded in an S shape between tall trees, so that it debouched abruptly into an open space at one side of which the three-storied mansion rose in ungraceful, indeed ungainly geometry. In the open space stood five big cars which Rogas instantly recognized from the size, color, and the license plates bearing State Service initials (for he knew nothing about makes and models) as official government cars. The five chauffeurs were standing together in a group. One of them was in uniform: an Air Corps sergeant. Drawing nearer, Rogas singled out and recognized among the five the chauffeur of the High Commissioner of Police. He was in mufti, but he gave Rogas a military salute.

Inside another cage, this one all glass, in the middle of the entrance hall, sat yet another porter. Again Rogas showed his identification card, said that he had come to speak with President Riches. Could His Excellency receive him? The porter shut the window of the cage and

75

spoke into the intercom. He reopened the window and advised that the President could receive no one at that moment; in any case, calls had to be announced in advance, confirmed in advance. "May I hope," Rogas said, with a touch of irony, "that the President will receive me tomorrow at this time?" "You may hope," the porter said sourly. He noted down on a slip of paper: "President Riches, Police Inspector, tomorrow, 5 P.M." "Thank you," Rogas said; and involuntarily, out of habitual curiosity, he added a question: "These gentlemen"—he gestured toward the automobiles outside—"are with the President?"

The porter looked at him with waspish suspicion. He countered with a second question: "Why do you want to know?" and closed the window to the cage again. He expected no reply, nor did he want one. His "why" had been purely punitive: there could be no "because" for the curiosity of a little police inspector about persons so much more powerful, with whose power the porter felt he was osmotically invested. To himself, Rogas said, "Why indeed?" Not about his own curiosity but about that meeting.

Once more he passed by the little group of chauffeurs, and once more he received the salute of the Commissioner's driver. Why indeed? The High Commissioner of Police . . . A high-ranking officer in the Air Corps . . . And the other three cars? That the High Commissioner of Police should have reason to confer with the President of the Supreme Court—nothing surprising about that. On the contrary, normal, standard, routine. Normal, however, in an office; a little less than normal at home. But an Air Corps officer? Unless he

76

were a judge advocate. But why the two of them, High Commissioner of Police and judge advocate? And the other three?

He went out through the iron gate. The street, rather narrow, was one-way. He walked a hundred feet or so, as far as the bus terminal.

From that terminal, the bus left only every hour: the area was inhabited by people who had no need of it. It had not yet arrived. Rogas pulled out his paper, opened it to the literary supplement. There was a piece about the translation of a Moravia novel, a Solzhenitsyn short story, essays by Lévi-Strauss, Sartre, Lukács. Translation, translation, nothing but translation. He tried to read, but with every automobile that passed he raised his eyes from the paper. He had decided, without deciding, to wait for the five official cars to pass by to see who was inside; it could well be that inside would be the wives of those powerful men, because official cars were used more by them than by their husbands. It was likely, in fact, that it would turn out to be the wives. A meeting of high-ranking wives would be more logical, more obvious, than a meeting of their husbands. But no, President Riches was a bachelor and a misogynist; it was to be excluded, then, that he would be receiving ladies.

The bus arrived hours later; that is, with the delay that customarily confronted travelers in that country, even if they were taking planes. Luckily, this time, for a person would have drawn attention to himself if he remained at the terminal, letting the bus leave without him. Thus Rogas saw the five automobiles pass by, at about five-minute intervals one from the other. Five times five, twenty-five: twenty-five minutes that were within the bus's delay. But why not together, one right after the other? Precaution? Concern? Against what? Over what?

In addition to his superior, Rogas recognized inside one of the automobiles the Commanding General of the National Gendarmerie, and he thought he recognized the Minister for Foreign Affairs crouched down into a corner of another car as if to make it appear empty. The other two he did not recognize, but in the automobile driven by the Air Corps sergeant there must have been a general from the same branch of the armed forces, even if he were dressed in civilian clothes. Stupidity typical of a general, Rogas thought: he takes the precaution of dressing in civies, and has himself driven by a chauffeur in military uniform.

When the bus arrived, Rogas stumbled aboard, very weary. While he had been absorbed in his thoughts, he hadn't noticed any fatigue. Now he felt it, even in his head. But he had developed the ability, when an idea became almost an obsession, to put it firmly out of his mind. The literary supplement to the newspaper helped him banish all other thoughts for the entire evening.

The next day, he was summoned urgently by the High Commissioner of Police, whose expression was dark and threatening. Without responding to the salute, letting Rogas remain standing, he said abruptly, "Yesterday you went to the home of the President of the Supreme Court. Why?"

Rogas explained why. The Commissioner's lowering expression was diluted with mockery. "With your infallible nose"—charging the infallible with being fallible—"you are still pursuing your Cres."

78

"Not exactly," Rogas said. "I am pursuing the possibility, which from one moment to the next could become fact, that an attempt will be made on the life of President Riches—on the part of my Cres or your cadres."

"The President is well guarded," the Commissioner replied.

"I know. But I should like, if you are not against it, to have a talk with him."

"Because you aren't willing to put that Cres out of your mind; there's the truth of the matter. Anyhow, go see the President; he's expecting you this afternoon. He telephoned me last evening. He told me you'd come in the afternoon but that he hadn't been able to see you. Also, that the porter had mentioned to him certain questions of yours. He was quite put out, you know."

"Only one question," Rogas said. And he thought, Now we're in for it.

"All right, only one. But indiscreet."

"Seeing your car, I thought you might have gone to the President for the same reason that I—"

"There were other official cars. Did you think we were all with President Riches for the same reason?"

"The other cars didn't interest me."

"No?" the Commissioner said, with sardonic disbelief.

"No. I asked about all of them because I didn't want to pinpoint my curiosity for the porter's benefit."

"However that may be, we were not all at Riches's. The Italian Ambassador, who lives in the same building, had invited us to a small afternoon reception. You know how the Italians are. They live in the expectation of being, so to speak, snubbed; they're quick to take offense. . . ."

79

"I understand," Rogas said.

"So go see the President. And please, be discreet." He made a gesture of dismissal and turned his attention to the papers lying before him.

Naturally, Rogas checked immediately. He went to a phone booth, closed the door, looked up and dialed the number of the Italian Ambassador (and he actually did reside in the same building as the President). He was about to hang up when an irritated voice answered. "Excuse me," Rogas said, "but General Fabert thinks he forgot a small portfolio at the Ambassador's home yesterday." "Who? When?" "General Fabert, yesterday afternoon." "Where?" "With you, at the Ambassador's home." "Look here, the Ambassador has been on vacation for two weeks; his apartment is closed. I happen to be here at the moment by chance. Your General What's-His-Name probably left his portfolio at the Embassy." "I think so, too. Thank you." He hung up, content.

Lunchtime had come, and Rogas set out for Thursday's restaurant; he had one for every day of the week—seven, then, that thought of him as a good client but not so faithful, so settled in, that they could give him poor service. Like every self-respecting investigator—that is, every investigator who entertains the same respect for himself that he wishes to arouse in his readers—Rogas lived alone; nor were there women in his life. (It seems —it seemed vaguely to him, too—that he might once have had a wife.)

He sat down at his customary table in the corner, chose food and wine with care. But he ate listlessly, absent-mindedly. Within the initial problem of a series of crimes that he, because of his duty, because of his profes-

80

sion, felt called upon to solve, whose author he must try to bring to court if not to justice, another problem had arisen, supremely criminal in kind—a crime contemplated in respect to fundamental principles of State, but one that would have to be solved outside the confines of his duty, in conflict with his duty. Practically, it was a matter of defending the State against those who represented it, who held it captive. The imprisoned State must be liberated. But he, too, was in prison: he could only try to open a crack in the wall.

He thought of his friend Cusan and of going to spend the evening with him, after his conversation with President Riches.

As he left the restaurant, the idea suddenly occurred to him that the Commissioner, immediately after dismissing him, had certainly picked up the phone to arrange to have him shadowed. Elementary—he should have thought of it before. And he felt he was being watched by someone; those eyes interfered with his walking, they mired him. He refrained from stopping in front of shopwindows, even when he was attracted by them, because stopping in front of shopwindows is typical of the person who fears or knows he is being shadowed. He went home, strenuously resisting the temptation to look behind him. He spent an hour shaving and reading desultorily. As he came out of the elevator and started to leave the building, he saw, beyond the glass door, on the pavement opposite, the man who had shadowed him. According to the rules, another man would follow him now; he would discover the new tail on the bus. And, in fact, he did discover him: at the terminal a furtive glance, as he was stepping down from the bus, was enough.

The man followed him as far as the outer gate to the park. He walked on ahead, naturally; without seeing him, Rogas could count his footsteps, draw the map of his movements. He would walk a hundred and fifty feet and he would turn back, but without entering the gate; he would go in search of a telephone, put in a call for his relief; then he would wait in front of the gate, making himself as inconspicuous as he could. Dog eat dog, Rogas thought. But there are dogs and dogs.

In the glass-walled cage in the middle of the entrance hall, the porter, because of the light, looked like a shark who was rushing against the walls of its tank. He recognized Rogas. He raised three fingers toward him: third floor.

On the third floor, one of four doors opened as Rogas stepped out of the elevator. A servant in a striped jacket, assuredly a police agent (or an ex-agent, given the age he looked to be), wordlessly ushered him into a spacious, well-ordered room. At the far end, in a corner armchair, behind a pale-blue cloud of smoke, sat the President. He said, "Come in," and when Rogas was near him, pointed to a chair: "Sit down."

Rogas saluted, sat down. The President peered at him over his glasses, acerb and caustic. Twice he drew on his cigar, puffing the smoke toward a ray of light that diffused it like a veil. Then slowly, contemptuously, he, invulnerable and immortal before the vulnerable, mortal little philistine, said, "So you believe they will kill me."

"I believe they will try."

"The cadres or that fellow who, according to you, was

82

the victim of a mistake? Of a judicial error, as it is usually termed." As he pronounced the words "judicial error," he made the syllables grate, like a blade against a whetstone, throwing off sparks of disdain.

"That fellow. Cres."

"Cres, that's it. . . . He had tried to do away with his wife. A rather ingenious plan, I'd say, but one of those that easily manage— What sentence did he get?"

"Five years in the court of first instance, confirmed by you on appeal."

"Not by me," the President said, placing his open hands before his chest and moving them out toward Rogas as if to repulse a disagreeable impact.

"Excuse me, I meant by the court over which you were presiding."

"That's right: by the court over which I was presiding." With condescending satisfaction, like a teacher who has at last got an acceptable reply from a dull student. "And so?"

"It was an error. A judicial error, as it is usually termed."

"Which is to say?"

"He was innocent."

"Really!"

"I believe so."

"He was innocent or you believe he was innocent?"

"I believe he was innocent. I can't be sure of it."

"Ah, you can't be sure of it!" Smiling, sardonic, from the summit of his certainties.

"I only think, not absolutely and indeed with a margin of doubt, that he was unjustly found guilty."

" 'Not absolutely, a margin of doubt' . . . That's amusing." And passing from the sardonic to the tragic, as if assailed by a sudden pain in the middle of the chest: "Have you ever thought about the problem of passing judgment on a man?" For a moment, he threw himself back in his chair, as if he were in the throes of death because of that problem.

"Constantly," Rogas said.

"Have you solved it?"

"No."

"Exactly, you have not solved it. . . . I have, obviously. . . . But not once and for all, not definitively . . . Here and now, speaking with you, and mindful of the next case whose outcome I shall have to preside over, I can even say I have not solved it. But, mind you, I am speaking of the next case. Not about the case that has just ended for me or about a case from ten or twenty or thirty years ago. For all the cases in the past, I solved the problem, always; and I solved it by the very fact of judging them, in the act of judging them. . . . You are a practicing Catholic?"

"No."

"But Catholic?"

Rogas made a gesture that signified: like everyone else. And in fact he did believe that all men everywhere were a little bit Catholic.

"Of course, like everyone else," the President interpreted correctly. Assuming the posture of a priest at catechism: "Let us take, well, the Mass, the mystery of transubstantiation, the bread and the wine that become the body, blood, soul, and divinity of Christ. The priest may even be unworthy in his personal life, in his thoughts. But the fact that he has been ordained means that at each celebration of the Mass the mystery is completed. Never, I say never, can it happen that the transubstantiation not take place. And so it is with a judge when he celebrates the law: justice cannot *not* be revealed, not transubstantiated, not completed. A judge may torment himself, wear himself out, tell himself, 'You are unworthy; you are full of meanness, burdened by passions, confused in your ideas, liable to every weakness and every error'—but in the moment when he celebrates the law, he is so no longer. And much less so afterward. Can you imagine a priest who, after celebrating Mass, says to himself, 'Who knows if the transubstantiation took place this time, too?' There's no doubt; it did take place. Most assuredly. I would even say inevitably. Think of that priest who was seized by doubt and who, at the moment of the consecration, discovered blood on his vestments. I can say this: no judgment has ever bloodied my hands, has ever stained my robes. . . ."

Without meaning to, Rogas made a sound much like a groan. The President looked at him with disgust. And as in a fireworks display, when everything seems to be over, in the stunned silence and darkness one more luminous, elaborate, and thunderous rocket explodes, Riches said, "Naturally, I am not a Catholic. Naturally, I am not even a Christian."

"Naturally," Rogas echoed. And indeed he was not surprised.

The President was disappointed and irritated, like someone who has just performed a magic turn only to have a child jump up and say he has understood the trick. With a note of hysteria, he proclaimed, "Judicial error does not exist."

"But the different levels of courts, the possibility of petitions, of appeals—" Rogas objected.

"—postulate, you mean to say, the possibility of error. But this is not so. They postulate merely an opinion—let us call it a lay opinion—about justice, about the administration of justice. An outside opinion. Now, when a religion begins to take lay opinion into account, it is already dead even if it doesn't know it. And so it is with justice, with the administration of justice. I use the term 'administration' to please you, clearly, and without granting it the slightest statutory or bureaucratic meaning." More subdued and persuasive now, and even melancholy: "Everything began with Jean Calas. . . . More or less, I mean. . . . Since we must establish definite points—a name, a date—when we try to apprehend the great defeats and the great victories of mankind. . . ."

"It began with—?"

"Jean Calas . . . 'The murder of Calas, committed in Toulouse with the sword of justice, on March 9, 1762, is one of the most remarkable events that deserve the attention of our age and of posterity. Soon forgotten is the numberless multitude of those who die in wars, not only because those dead belong to an inevitable fatality but also because they were in condition to visit death upon their enemies and not to fall without having defended themselves. There where the danger and the advantage are equal, pained astonishment ceases and even pity is weakened; but if the innocent father of a family falls into the clutches of error, or of passion, or of fanaticism; if the accused has no defense other than his own virtue; if the arbiters of his life run no other risk, ordering his throat to be cut, than that of being wrong; if they can kill with impunity through a sentence, then the public voice is raised, everyone fears for himself. . . .' Have you ever read it?"

"*An Essay on Tolerance, Upon the Occasion of the Death of Jean Calas,*" Rogas recited.

"Ah, you have read it," the President remarked. Banteringly, but with an undertone of menace: "Our police permit themselves unimaginable luxuries."

"I permit myself some reading," Rogas amended.

"And the police permit themselves to have you on the force. But let's let that go. . . . Jean Calas, then . . . The *Essay,* and everything else Voltaire wrote about the death of Calas, I know almost by heart. It was the starting point of error—the error of believing there could exist such a thing as judicial error. . . . Naturally, this error does not spring out of nothing, nor does it remain like that, isolated or at least isolatable; there is soil, there is a context for it to grow in. . . . I've spent a great deal of my life, an infinity of those hours one calls free—free from the burdens of office, and for me there are never any free hours in that sense of the word—in confuting Voltaire about the case of Jean Calas. That is, in refuting the idea of justice, of the administration of justice, which, so Voltaire assumes, was belied in that case." He pointed to a thick stack of notebooks on the table. "There it is. My refutation, my essay."

"Will you publish it?" The same question he had, a few days before, put to Vilfredo Nocio.

Unlike Nocio, the President was not horrified. "Certainly I will publish it. As soon as conditions prevail that will favor its success. And I do not speak, quite obviously, of material, practical success. I am speaking of an ideal success. . . . I'd say the time is not far off. . . . Because, you see, the advent of the masses is the condition that allows us to turn back and to start out again on the right foot. Follow my reasoning. . . ." He edged forward in his chair, leaned toward Rogas with a winning smile, his eyes bright with a feverish anxiety. The way it happens in asylums, Rogas thought, where you always run into the man who stops you to confide in you about his Utopia, his Civitas Dei, his phalanstery. "Now follow my line of reasoning. . . . The weak point in Voltaire's tract, the point where I take off to set things right again, occurs on the very first page, when he proposes the difference between death in war and death at the hands, let us say, of justice. This difference does not exist; justice sits in a perennial state of danger, in a perennial state of war. It was so also in Voltaire's day, but it was not perceived, and in any event, Voltaire was too gross to realize it. But now it is perceived. What earlier could be gleaned by a subtle mind the masses have made macroscopic; they have brought human existence to a total and absolute state of war. I'll risk a paradox that can also be a prophecy: the only possible form of justice, of the administration of justice, could be, and will be, the form that in a military war is called decimation. One man answers for humanity. And humanity answers for the one man. No other way of administering justice will be possible. I'll go further: there never has been any other. But the moment is coming to give this fact theoretical expression, to codify it. To prosecute a guilty man, guilty men, is impossible—practically, technically impossible. It's no longer a question of looking for the needle in the haystack, but of looking in the haystack for one single straw. Among other idiocies in circulation, someone said once that it is impossible to remember the face of a Chinese because all Chinese look alike. Then it was noticed that at least three faces of Chinese are unforgettable, and they do not look alike. But millions of men, hundreds of millions of men do look alike—I don't say physically. Or, rather, not only physically. There are no more individuals; there are no more individual responsibilities. Your profession, my dear friend, has become absurd. It presupposes the existence of the individual, and the individual does not exist. It presupposes the existence of God, the God who blinds some men and enlightens others, the God who hides—and has remained hidden so long that we may presume Him dead. It presupposes peace, and there is war. . . . This is the point: war. . . . War exists, and dishonor and crime must be restored to the corpus of the multitude the way in military wars it is restored to regiments, divisions, armies. Punished by lot. Tried by fate."

"Number can never be indefinite," Rogas said.

"How's that? What did you say?"

Rogas did not answer. He was trying to remember how it went: *"Argumentum ornithologicum.* I close my eyes and see a flock of birds. The vision lasts a second or perhaps less. I don't know how many birds I saw. Were they a definite or indefinite number? This problem involves the question of the existence of God. If God exists, the number is definite, because how many birds I saw is known to God. If God does not exist, the number is indefinite, because nobody was able to take count. In this case, I saw fewer than ten birds (let's say) and more than one; but I did not see nine, eight, seven, six, five, four, three, or two. I saw a number somewhere between ten and one, but not nine, eight, seven, six, five, etc. That number, as a whole number, is inconceivable; *ergo,* God exists." When the brief page had reconstituted itself in his memory as it is reproduced here, he turned from it to give his attention once more to what the President was saying, but with the sense that that flock of birds, which for a second or maybe less had flown before Borges's closed eyes, might be much more real, not to say definite, than the man who was talking to him and than everything else around him.

The President, continuing that part of his dissertation which Rogas did not regret having missed, was saying, "For that matter, the problem of justice, for Voltaire and those who descend from him, seems to converge on those crimes he calls local—*délits locaux.* But today the masses, running roughshod over legal codes like a thirsty herd—thirsting for crime, I mean—have trampled local crimes underfoot. The judge need no longer ask himself, 'Would I dare punish in Ragusa what I punish in Loreto?' What is punished in Ragusa *is* punished in Loreto. But it would be more accurate to speak of what is *not* punished. . . . Few things are punished, at this point."

"It doesn't seem so to me," Rogas said. "And as for local crimes, Loreto is in Italy; Ragusa now calls itself Dubrovnik, and is in Yugoslavia. One can't say that what is punished in Italy is necessarily punished in Yugo-slavia."

"Maybe not, maybe not." With an air of absent-minded skepticism.

"You don't think so?"

"If you really want to know, no. Because you are making the mistake of considering local those crimes which are instead universal and eternal—in other words, everywhere and always punished. Those crimes against the legitimacy of authority that only authority, by reversing itself and taking the perpetrators' part, can cancel out as crimes and transform into acts of witness for the entrance of God into the world, presupposing that this reverse authority is unalterably ready to receive Him. . . . The only entrance the world allows God. . . . Not the God who hides Himself, of course. Now, it is precisely these crimes, the way in which these crimes have always been judged and punished—the method, the procedure —that offers secure elements to my treatise. In trials of this type, the guilt has been, and is, prosecuted with the most total disregard for the accused individual's pleas of innocence. Whether an accused man may or may not have committed the crime has never had any importance for judges. . . ."

"But the fact that in such trials one tries by every means to obtain the defendant's confession to a crime he has not committed—"

"You are saying exactly the opposite of what you mean. . . . You remember that famous pamphlet attacking the trial in Milan, in 1630, in which persons were accused of spreading the plague with unctions? The author, an Italian Catholic, says the trial lays bare an injustice that could readily have been seen by the very people who perpetrated it—by the judges, that is. Well, of course they saw it! They would not have been judges if they hadn't seen it. But even less would they have been judges had their seeing it led them to absolve rather than

91

to convict. No matter that the organized, institutional-ized unleashing of a plague was not morally conceivable, *ergo* not possible then—whereas today, as we know, it is. And no matter that a motive was lacking with which to charge the defendants, that there was not a glimmer of proof, and that even circumstantial clues did not tally. There was the plague; this is the point. The fellow who denied it—actually a character created by the author of the pamphlet—in point of fact represented the one lay attitude then possible. Ridiculous, naturally. But Voltaire, a hundred years later, is no less so. And likewise, two hundred years after Voltaire, Bertrand Russell and Sartre."

"But confession—"

"If you give a religious rather than a technical sense to the word, confession of a misdeed on the part of some-one who has not committed it establishes what I call the circuit of legitimacy. That religion is true, that power is legitimate, which brings man into a state of guilt; guilty in body, in mind. And from the state of guilt it is easy to abstract the elements for the conviction of crime, easier than from objective proofs, which, for that matter, do not exist. On the contrary, if anything, it is objective proofs that can give rise to what you call judicial error."

"Exactly, in the case in question it was the objective proofs that gave rise to error. Cres was found guilty—"

"It doesn't interest me," the President said.

"I understand," Rogas said. "I understand very well. But you see, Your Excellency, it is my job to look for the single straw in the haystack, as you so well put it. And that straw is armed, it shoots, it has already murdered some seven high officials—to this point without making

92

a false step, without ever being diverted. Now, I am willing also to admit that I may be wrong, that the attacks may come from some other quarter. There remains nonetheless the problem of assuring you adequate protection, enough to frustrate the plan of Cres or of the cadres. . . . Do you consider yourself sufficiently protected, sufficiently safe?"

A shadow of fear passed over the face of the President.

"What do you think?" he asked, with an arrogance tempered by anxiety, an anxiety masked by arrogance.

"I think that you will be as protected and as safe as possible so long as you feel unprotected, unsafe."

"Ah," the President said, impressed.

Like a sleepwalker, Rogas found himself once again in the elevator; in the entrance hall, as the gates swung quickly open, he had the sensation for a moment of finding himself before a mirror. Except that in the mirror was another man.

"Excuse me," the other man said, entering the elevator as Rogas left it.

"Not at all," Rogas said. Suddenly alert, tensed, senses and memory exploding within him in the most delicate tentacles. His same build, five feet eight inches tall: therefore, the sensation of the mirror on finding himself suddenly face to face in the artificial light of the entrance hall. Very dark-skinned, in contrast to the white hair. Slightly bald. Slightly aquiline nose? Maybe not. Not exactly thin: robust, healthy. He had put on a little weight, his hair seemed whiter; he had perhaps had plastic surgery done on his nose. But what identity had he assumed? How had he managed to get entrée into the building where, among other powerful personages, President Riches lived?

Rogas controlled his own impulses—with no excessive effort, it must be said to his credit or discredit, as you prefer. The sudden temptation to reënter the elevator, to return to the President's apartment, came as a flash that was immediately quenched in the recollection—rather cynical, given the circumstances—of what Innocent says as he aims the revolver at the Schopenhauer professor (G. K. Chesterton, *Man Alive*): "It's not a thing I'd do for everyone. But you and I seem to have got so intimate to-night, somehow." The remark aimed now at the President, of course, with whom the revolver of Cres was perhaps at that moment about to settle accounts. The phrase, visually repeating itself in an elegant italic, made a kind of selvage edge to his ruminations, and it was fading into rhythm, into music ("It's-not-a-thing-I'd-do-for-everyone," to the theme of a shower song; and then, "But-you-and-I-seem-to-have-got-so-intimate," in a broad Puccinian phrase, baritone air, and timbre), when he realized that he had already been on the bus for some time, that the street lights in the city had come on, haloed by the sirocco, that shops were closing, that he was therefore no longer in time to give his tail the slip by dragging him along behind, as he had planned, into a big store (Square Deal) where the many doors, elevators, escalators, and, above all, the crowd allowed one to confuse the most skillful operative of the police or of the Center of Special Information. Because, according to Rogas, the two who had first followed him were from the police, but the man who was following him now, and who in the almost empty bus had planted himself so that he

94

could not be caught off guard by his quarry's suddenly departing, was certainly from the C.S.I.; it was evident from the good cut of his clothes, his short hair, his well-fed appearance. Unlike Americans of the same calling, whom they considered models and tried to emulate, C.S.I. agents indulged more than they should in good food (expense-account funds) and less in the gymnastics and sports prescribed by their order on the same frequency as prayers by Benedictines.

The agent opened the evening paper he was holding, and Rogas glanced at the headlines: another judge had been killed.

He suddenly remembered a detail: Cres was carrying a small traveling case. And from that detail there flowed a deduction: the man had not gone into the mansion to kill the President but because he lived there. He was coming back from a trip, that was it—from the city where, a few hours earlier, he had succeeded in doing away with one more judge. He could kill the President whenever he wanted to, but the cover of living in that building was so perfect that, in order not to compromise it, surely he was postponing, and would continue to postpone, the decision to act. But perhaps more than the security and invisibility he had managed to create for himself, what counted with Cres in keeping the President alive were considerations of order, of planning; for these reasons he was holding the President in reserve, as if on a game preserve or in a hen coop, for the final banquet.

His sudden discovery of Cres, who had found the most comfortable and privileged asylum under the same roof as the President of the Supreme Court, disquieted Rogas. Professional eagerness, impatience to verify, to make sure, were combined with the fear that, in that fleeting encounter, Cres might have recognized him: in his uncertainty whether the Inspector might have discovered his refuge or, in the casual and rapid meeting, might have been brushed by a suspicion or even by only an impression, he would disappear again, renouncing his plan to put the President to death or deferring it to a better time. But there would never *be* a better time to kill the President. Only, if Cres had recognized the Inspector and believed he had been recognized in turn, he could never imagine that that police inspector, who, the papers said, was tenaciously but vainly tracking him down, had actually passed over to his side. Nevertheless, like an aficionado who sits before his television and enjoys (or suffers through) a football game, anticipating, imploring, calling for the decisive play, the impetuous descent on the opposing team's field, the winning pass, Rogas was turning over in his mind what, in Cres's place, he would do, what Cres should do. Meanwhile he wanted to be sure that he had not made a mistake, that the man really was Cres. Go back and ask information from the porters and the agents? Look up the manager of the building? But if Cres really lived there, there was the risk of his coming to know about Rogas's inquiry and then of his taking fright and running away.

At the Clio Square stop, Rogas indolently stepped down from the bus. He bought a paper. The news report on the judge's murder, in boldface, was brief. Turning the pages of the paper, he walked along under the arcade. The C.S.I. agent seemed to have disappeared, but Rogas knew that he was standing in the least illuminated area of the square.

He went into a café, ordered a cup of cold milk and one of hot coffee. He sugared each, drank them in quick succession. The two opposed and almost simultaneous sensations, cold, hot, canceled each other out, and for a few moments his body acquired a kind of imperviousness to the terrible pall of the sirocco which was descending on the city. Then a good idea came to him. The café was nearly deserted, and the telephone was well placed to prevent any curious person from coming close without being noticed. Rogas dialed the number (secret) of President Riches. As he foresaw, the butler answered. He said, "I am Inspector Rogas. I'm calling to ask you some routine information. . . . Yes, you. . . . I would never dream of disturbing His Excellency. . . . Yes. . . . So, I should like to have the names of the people living in the building: their names and, if possible, some information about their activities, their professions. . . . The Ambassador of Italy, then; the president of National Radio-Television; the Duke of Lieva; Mr. Ribeiro, Carlos Ribeiro . . . Spanish? . . . Ah, Portuguese. And what does Mr. Ribeiro do? Is he with the Portuguese Embassy? . . . No, if you don't mind, let's pause a moment over Mr. Ribeiro. What's he like? Physically, I mean. . . . Ah, a fine-looking man . . . very good . . . Let's go on. . . ." This simply so as not to arouse the suspicions of the butler, ex-police agent, about his special interest in Mr. Ribeiro.

So Cres had taken the name of Ribeiro. A Portuguese businessman. Portuguese face. Portuguese passport. And wealthy like a wealthy Portuguese.

The next morning, standing a long time under the shower, Rogas made up his program for the day. But the program could be carried out only if he managed to shake the agents who were tailing him. Because from now on all the people he met would automatically come under surveillance also, and who knew for how long and with what consequences.

He stayed in his office for several hours to write a report on his visit to President Riches. He put into the account all the irony that none of the people who would read it would be able to grasp—the whole hierarchy through whose hands it would pass, the future archives researcher, the historian. A world unsuited for irony, but Rogas was nonetheless amused to employ it. He closed the report thus: "From the moment the undersigned left the home of the President of the Supreme Court, he has had the clear impression of being shadowed by experts —that is, by persons particularly fitted for such an assignment, as if they might have been trained in an official or private police corps. If higher echelons have taken the trouble to make such arrangements for the protection of the undersigned, the undersigned can only express his appreciation but at the same time permit himself to observe that such vigilance, so costly because of the employment of so many men who work in shifts, would be better directed toward the protection of judges. If, however, higher echelons have not ordered the surveillance and are completely unaware of it, the undersigned deems it would be opportune, and indeed absolutely necessary, to take measures whereby equally able police agents devote themselves to tailing the tails."

The time had come for the daily report that the Chief of the Political Section received from the subordinates in his office. But that day there was no report; the Chief of

Section, a colleague informed Rogas, was questioning a girl who was one of the most active members of a cadre on the rampage in the city where the day before a judge had been killed. She had been brought to the capital by plane, together with three companions; the Chief of Section had wished to start with her. Because she is a woman, Rogas thought. And, Will he beat her with a flower?

He peeped into the waiting room; three young people were waiting to be questioned, and a dozen policemen were guarding them. Bearded, jacketless, with contemptuous glances and smiles for the fuzz, the three did not talk and did not even look at each other. Poor things, he thought: not because they were about to meet an idiot, not because they were living through that little scrape (in a few hours, they would be free, toasted by their friends and virtually awarded decorations and patents of nobility for their day spent in captivity). He pitied them, he pitied all young people whenever he found them caged in their scorn, their anger. Not that there was nothing to be angry and scornful about. But there was also something to laugh about.

He went downstairs and out into the square. It was the hour when traffic tangled the city in a fierce snarl. He struck off on foot, since finding a taxi was out of the question. For a quarter of an hour, at a brisk pace, he walked under the sun; finally, he turned in to Frazer Street, tranquil, bordered by a fringe of shade. It was a long, straight avenue, closed to traffic in both directions. Rich people lived here, not recently rich people but those whose money dated back to a time when wealth was at least converted into decorum (*Deco*, in this case).

99

He entered No. 30: here lived three generations of Pattoses, shipowners, proprietors of the newspaper *The Star*, friends of the High Commissioner of Police ("Report to me tomorrow, for this evening I'm having dinner with the Pattoses"). Rogas, on the other hand, enjoyed the friendship of the porter; he had proved the man's innocence once when the police were firmly intent on charging him with a big robbery at the Pattoses' residence. Cutting the effusions short, Rogas rapidly explained to the porter what he should do: pretend to speak over the intercom with the masters of the house, who were on vacation, as if he were announcing a call; accompany Rogas to the elevator; wait until the gentleman out on the street (not there yet but sure to appear in a second) came to ask about him, about whom he had gone to see; tell the man that he had gone to call on old Mr. Pattos. The tail turned up as the porter was talking into the house phone (he was simply reëvoking the trouble from which Rogas had rescued him). He hung up and arose to accompany Rogas to the elevator. Rogas went up to the second floor and then walked down the stairs. He placed himself so as to hear, without being seen, the dialogue between the C.S.I. agent and the porter.

"That gentleman who went in just now, whom did he go to see?"

"Why do you want to know?" The habitual counterquestion.

"Just curiosity," the agent said, coldly threatening.

"He went to see Mr. Pattos."

"Pattos who?"

"Pattos Pattos," the porter said, with a certain pride.

"The shipowner?"

"The shipowner."

"All right . . . When he comes down, don't tell him someone was here asking questions. Clear?"

"Clear."

He left. And Rogas left, too, walking through the cellar and coming out into Pirenne Street, parallel to but not connected with Frazer Street. To catch up with him, the C.S.I. agent would have had to walk an extra half mile, but at that moment the suspicion did not occur to him that Rogas might have escaped him; he was relishing the importance of the information he had just learned, which would be immediately communicated to his principals; one does not go to see important people except on important matters.

From a café, Rogas placed one call to Cusan, making an appointment to meet him in a restaurant outside of town, and a second call to a taxi stand for a cab to come and pick him up. A half hour later, he was sitting under a pergola, sipping a well-chilled white wine. Cusan's being late was a small advantage: it allowed him to sort out his facts, hypotheses, conjectures. He reordered them lucidly in the cool of the breeze filtering through the vine leaves, in the cool of the wine, but there was an undercurrent of apprehension, of insecurity, perhaps of fear.

He told Cusan everything.

Cusan was a committed writer; therefore, to find himself in any way responsible for those secrets, those dangers, plunged him into consternation. But he was an honest man, a loyal friend. After trying, from every angle and at every weak point, to demolish Rogas's castle of impressions, deductions, hypotheses, he realized that he

101

was trapped inside it together with Rogas, as if they were in a labyrinth and must find the thread in order to get out. One thread lay within reach: the one that would lead them out by their simply forgetting. More than once, in their thoughts, they brushed by this thread; each was on the point of grasping it. The pleasure of the place, the food, the wine; the dear, good paternal and maternal figures repeating the who-says-you-must-do-it? formula that two thousand years of their country's history made prophetic and fatal; the memories of a carefree youth that always crowded their meetings; the longing for things still to be understood, a world still to be seen, books still to be read in the perspective of a maturity and a serenity they felt they were approaching (cancer or embolism permitting)—everything converged to turn their minds toward that thread of salvation, of oblivion. But neither mentioned it to the other, and each was ashamed to be thinking of it yet not to speak of it, although they would have been even more ashamed to speak of it. But also concealed under will and conscience was the cowardly reciprocal anticipation that the other would give in.

Cusan did give in a little when, both having arrived at the most obvious solution, he volunteered for the mission that had to be carried out. In his tone of voice rather than in his words, there were almost imperceptible nuances of resignation and, at the same time, of heroism. And the more he insisted, the more reasons he adduced that made him suitable for the mission, the more perceptible the nuances became.

"I know Amar very well. I'm sure that he thinks well of me, that he trusts me. . . . Also, I can approach him without arousing suspicion. . . . A writer goes to see the Secretary-General of the International Revolutionary Party: nothing merits greater inattention on the part of the police or the C.S.I. What can a writer want from Amar? A literary prize, the good will of the Party paper? And what can Amar want from a writer? A signature on a manifesto of protest, a statement about this or that suppressed freedom, this or that right that's been trampled on? . . . No risk for me. Whereas you . . ."

Rogas said no, he continued to say no. "I'll go see Amar. Tomorrow. And I'll find the safest way. It's my job. A hunter who casts himself in the role of the hare is certainly better able than the hare to stay clear of trouble. . . . Don't worry. Tomorrow, after I've talked with Amar, I'll come see you—always assuming that I manage to get rid of my guardian angel."

"But if, before you go see Amar, you're not absolutely sure no one is following you, telephone me and *I'll* go," Cusan offered again.

"I'll get rid of him. As you see, I did today," and with his hand he made a gesture to include all the innocuous patrons in the restaurant garden who were lingering over the good wine and enjoying the cool breeze.

But he was mistaken. "One can be cleverer than another, not cleverer than all others." (La Bruyère?)

Rogas did not put in an appearance the next day, Saturday, nor on Sunday morning; that is, at the times when he was still able, in the literal sense of the phrase, to put in an appearance.

At midday Sunday, while Cusan was eating his lunch, he had the television in the next room turned on, as

103

usual, to hear something of the day's events without having to watch the gray, monotonous pictures, and thus he learned that Rogas was dead. The voice of the newscaster, with that tremolo of emotion and commotion reserved for earthquakes and air disasters, announced: "This morning at eleven o'clock, in a room in the National Gallery, a group of foreign visitors came upon the corpse of a man apparently in his forties. The police arrived promptly and identified the dead man as Inspector Americo Rogas, one of the corps's best-known and most able investigators, and quickly determined that the cause of death was three revolver shots. The Inspector was gripping his service pistol in his right hand. . . . But immediately after, police agents made another and far more serious discovery: In the adjoining room, also felled by gunshots, probably from the same weapon, lay the body of Amar, Secretary-General of the International Revolutionary Party." The toothachy face of the newscaster dissolved (Cusan was now standing before the TV screen). Next appeared the entrance to the National Gallery, the stairway, the succession of exhibit rooms. Room XII. A dark mass at the feet of a standing portrait. "The body of Mr. Amar was found under a famous portrait by Velázquez." Room XI. "The body of the Inspector of Police, under the painting of the Madonna of the Chair, by an unknown fifteenth-century Florentine artist. . . . This is how, on the basis of testimony and of hypotheses suggested by those investigating the crimes, the facts can be reconstructed." A terrified face appeared. "You were on duty this morning at the entrance to the museum. Did you see the two men who have been killed come in?" "I saw them come in. First the gentleman they say was a

104

police inspector arrived. About ten minutes later, the other one, Mr. Amar, arrived." "They were not together, then?" "No, definitely not." "Then what?" "Then a young man came, blond, tall, with a well-kept beard." "What kind of a beard?" "Short, fringed, I'd say." "How was he dressed?" "Black trousers, very tight-fitting. Embroidered shirt. He was carrying a small black pouch in one hand." "How soon after Mr. Amar did this blond young man with the beard arrive?" "Two, three minutes after." "Did anyone else come in?" "No one until about eleven, when the herd of Americans— Excuse me, but we call tourist parties herds, like that, as a joke." "Did you see the young man leave?" "Yes, a few minutes before the tourist group came in." "Was he upset, was he running?" "Not at all, he was very calm." "Tell me, if you were to meet him would you recognize him?" "By now, he would have shaved his beard. How can I recognize him without the beard?" And the man disappeared from the screen, grinning with relief. "Here now is the guard on the second floor of the museum." Worried face, nervous tic between eye and mouth. "And what did you see?" "Nothing. The three men walked by me, one after the other, in the order and at the time my colleague said." "Where were you?" "In the first room." "And you never moved away?" "Never." "You heard nothing?" "Nothing." "Did you see the young man as he left?" "I saw him." Dissolve. "Now let us hear from the police inspector who is in charge of the investigation. He is Dr. Blom, Chief of the Political Section. . . . Inspector, can you tell us why the investigation has been undertaken by the Political Section?" The Inspector's face, lined by bureaucratic tribulations and dyspepsia, broke into a commiserating smile. "Mr. Amar was a political man, and a political man is usually killed for political reasons." "Have you a precise idea about the political reasons for which he was killed?" "I have." "Naturally, at this juncture you cannot talk about them." "Naturally." "Can you tell us, at least, what, according to you, was the sequence of events?" "Well, we must assume that both Mr. Amar and my colleague Rogas, who as far as I can discover did not know each other, liked to visit galleries and museums in their free time. Mr. Amar was, as everyone knows, a cultivated man; also my colleague was considered by the rest of us to be a man of exceptional culture." This with a slight grimace, as if exceptional culture must finally, inevitably, be gunned down. And no more than right. "This morning, by chance, both happened, almost at the same time, to visit the National Gallery. I should say, to revisit, because each of them, their respective friends tell me, enjoyed looking at certain paintings again and again. Mr. Amar, for example, considered that the portrait by Velázquez, near which he was killed, was one of the masterpieces of world art. So they were both here. Rogas arrived first, then Mr. Amar. The gallery, as always in the early morning hours, was deserted. The third arrival was not, evidently, an art lover. He was following Mr. Amar (he entered the gallery a few minutes behind him), if not with a precise plan, then certainly with criminal intent. The gallery deserted, Mr. Amar, contrary to his habits, alone—what better opportunity to carry it out? He did not take into account the possibility that someone else could have entered the museum first. But this was a minor oversight, since, as far as the murderer was concerned, the presence of Rogas was resolved by commit-

106

ting a second crime. . . . According to me, Rogas was in Room XIV, or in Room XV, when he heard the shot fired in Room XII. . . . Very probably, the assassin's revolver was equipped with a silencer; therefore, the guard in the first room did not hear. But the sound did not escape Rogas, he being nearer and having a trained ear. He ran to Room XII, he saw the body of Mr. Amar. Then he drew his own revolver. And here a small question arises. When Rogas caught up with the assassin in the next room, did the assassin, who was still holding his gun in his hand, turn and fire three shots? Or, hearing someone arrive from the rooms up ahead, did he stand back against the wall, beside the door Rogas had to pass through, in order to shoot him down from behind? According to me, the second hypothesis is the correct one, but confirmation will come from the autopsy." The Inspector disappeared, the newscaster reappeared. His previously stricken face was now sculpted in a violent rictus of grief. "Before asking the Vice-Secretary-General of the International Revolutionary Party to speak, we must announce further fearful news: His Excellency Ernest Riches, President of the Supreme Court, has been murdered in his home. The assassin, who was able—how is not known—to gain access to the well-guarded residence, took advantage of the customary Sunday-morning absence of the President's old and faithful servant. . . . We will have further details during the two-o'clock news telecast."

Cusan knew by whom and how President Riches had been killed. He knew that Amar and Rogas had not been at the National Gallery by chance. And from what he knew, from what he believed he knew, he readily imagined that their meeting—what Rogas would have told Amar, what Amar would have set in motion on hearing Rogas's revelations—must be sealed in death. Of course, it was not impossible that the tall blond young man with the fringe of beard and the embroidered shirt was of the extraction which television and newspapers were shortly to hint at and then, with absolute certainty, affirm, and that he was following Amar in order to eliminate him at the most likely opportunity. But for Cusan it was easier to imagine—in fact, he felt it was indisputable—that the man being shadowed was Rogas; shadowed by a C.S.I. agent opportunely bearded and disguised, for there were surely a lot of them set loose among the cadres and in the heroin and LSD cult centers. Rogas must have had more than one agent tailing him, so, having eluded the first (and he would not have gone to the appointment if he had not been absolutely sure of having ditched him), he did not realize he had the second on his heels. At this point, Cusan felt, in the heat of the day and the hour, the cold sweat of fear. What if the same had been true yesterday, too, he thought, at his meeting with Rogas in the restaurant outside of town? Rogas had considered himself safe because he had given the slip to the agent who followed him to the Pattos house, but there could have been another one, and even more than one, in a car, ready to move in any direction. Nor would the trick of entering by the main door and leaving by a smaller door on another street have been such an impenetrable ploy for people like the C.S.I. operatives, who were capable of performing any and all shrewd stratagems and therefore quite up to foreseeing them. Maybe the maneuver

108

with the two doors was enough to elude the police. But not *them*. Already Cusan felt them diabolically omnipresent and omnipowerful, implacable lemurs who brushed by, slunk by, reeking of violence and death, fouling the elements of his own life. That Rogas. What a mess he'd dragged him into. But the rancor that welled up in Cusan immediately subsided to focus on one particular, one detail. Rogas used to do his job well, but he tended to disparage the tools that technology put at the disposal of his profession. Refusing to make use of them himself, he ended up forgetting that others did make use of them. What had finished him—what was about to finish him, Cusan—was perhaps a tiny receiving and transmitting radio, the kind that by now is to be found even in the toy departments of big stores.

Don't panic, he told himself. Poor Rogas. Poor Amar. This poor country of ours. Meanwhile, from behind the window curtain he was scrutinizing the sunny, deserted street as if it were the maw of a canyon: the silent ambush, the crack of the sniper's rifle striking down the explorer who ventured there. And suddenly he drew back from the window, for the sniper could be standing by the window opposite.

He was alone in the house; his wife and children were at the shore. Always alone in the difficult moments of his life. Which difficult moments? He searched for some that resembled the one he was living through now. But this was not a moment; it was the end. And with the thought of the end, of the death that was awaiting him in the canyon, slowly he regained a sense of quiet, perhaps even peace. Like a transparency beyond which actions, persons, things were encamped as if in quarantine. Disinfected. Antiseptic.

He became fearful again because the canyon was in shadow. "Now I'll write it all down," he said to himself.

He wrote for more than two hours. Reread it. Good. Very good. Maybe these are the only pages of mine that will survive: a document. He folded the document. Where do I put it? *Don Quixote, War and Peace, Remembrance of Things Past*? A book that would be saved, a book that would save the document.

He chose, naturally, *Don Quixote.* Then he wrote a note: "In my library, bookcase E, third shelf, between the pages of *Don Quixote,* a document concerning the death of Amar and Rogas. And mine." He slipped the note in an envelope. But to whom to address it? To his wife, to the Vice-Secretary-General of the Revolutionary Party, to the president of the Writers' Union? He thought also of the Abbot of St. Damian, for they had been friends in school. He finally decided to address it to himself. But he had to go out to post it.

He left the lamp on in his study, and did not light any others to reach the stairway. He walked down in the dark, went out. A few passersby; also, at the corner of the street, right by the letter box, two bodies, clutching each other and writhing. Cusan crossed over to the other pavement; when he was opposite to the couple, he stopped a moment to look at them, like a voyeur but actually scrutinizing them to distinguish in that tangle the real from the sham. He was reassured; sham could not be carried to those lengths. He crossed the street, dropped the letter in the box. Through a shock of hair and beard, one eye, hers or his, glinted with derision, as

110

if to say, "If you want to look, there's no need for the excuse of mailing a letter." Annoyed, Cusan thought, It's the libertines who are preparing the revolution, but it's the puritans who will make it. They, the two grapplers, the whole generation they belong to, would never make a revolution. Their children, maybe; and they would be puritans.

Reflecting on these things, he returned home. He was no longer afraid, but all the same he did not sleep.

The next day, he telephoned a friend, an erstwhile literary critic and theoretician of commitment (but a homemade commitment, like cookies for which the family hands down the recipe, and which seem an altogether different thing if one adds a dash more of salt or ginger or vanilla); the man was now an eminence, not gray but multicolored, nuanced, iridescent, in the cultural affairs of the Revolutionary Party. Cusan asked his friend to set up for him, with all possible urgency, a private appointment with the Vice-Secretary-General. "Go tomorrow to the funeral"—cultural politics—"and I'll be able to have some word for you." "Of course I'm going"—he still felt himself a committed writer—"but don't you forget to speak about this to the Vice-Secretary as soon as you can. It's about something urgent and very confidential."

He stayed in the house all day Monday. Tuesday, the funerals: Rogas's in the Church of San Rocco, filled with police and flags (poor Rogas); Amar's in the great hall of the Party's headquarters. There was a third, in the Palace of Justice: that of President Riches. The nation was in mourning, but the city, with the colors of the flags at half mast on a splendid summer day, seemed on holiday. Every now and then, people were seen suddenly to coagulate: citizens, lovers of law and order, were surrounding some rash person who had come out in beard and long hair to dispute his right to kill policemen, judges, and representatives of the Revolutionary Party, as well as, obviously, his right to exist. There were attempted lynchings; many persons, especially the blond-haired and bearded, ended up in the hospital, but there were no fatalities, thanks to the timely intervention of the forces of law and order against the lovers of law and order.

In the confusion and commotion that swirled around the coffin of Amar, Cusan was able for a moment to get to his friend and to hear from him "Tomorrow afternoon at five, here"—that is, at Party headquarters. After which, having acquitted himself of the obligation to be seen at the funeral, he went back home. He noted in the mailbox the letter he had sent himself. He left it there; his wife would be the one to pick it up, if there were reserved for him, before he met the Vice-Secretary of the Party, the same end as Rogas (poor Rogas). But now when he felt afraid he realized he was perhaps injecting a measure of pretense, of complacency, into his reactions; nonetheless, real desperate tremors crept in, especially when the furniture creaked or the windowpanes tinkled.

Wednesday afternoon, at four, he phoned for a taxi and had himself driven to the headquarters of the Revolutionary Party. He arrived, naturally, way in advance of the time set for the meeting; he walked up and down the

112

street with heroic, provocative slowness, waiting for the shot. It did not come.

At three minutes to five, he went in by the main door, crossed the main hall, climbed the great baroque staircase. He was still ruminating over the baroque when the Vice-Secretary came forward to meet him in the large, austere office that had been Amar's, and in which Amar appeared now only in a youthful portrait painted by one of the most prestigious artists who were militant activists in the Party.

"We still cannot believe it," the Vice-Secretary said, motioning toward the portrait. The classical phrase that mourners and condolers pronounce during visits of mourning. But he did believe it.

"Ah, yes, incredible," Cusan said.

Silence. Then the Vice-Secretary said, "I was waiting for you. . . . No, I don't mean now, not for this appointment our mutual friend set up. . . . I've been waiting for you, let's say, since Sunday evening. . . . Knowing your seriousness and your loyalty, your good will for our Party. . . . Amar admired you very much, you know? . . . I had no doubt, in a word, that sooner or later you would come to explain to us, to clarify for us—"

"But—"

"We knew that you'd met with that Rogas the day before he went to Amar—Saturday."

"Yes, I met with Rogas." Alarmed, he asked himself, Why "*that*" Rogas?

"We—let me be quite clear. We do not know this directly, but from information passed on to us by others. . . . And to these other persons we have said that we trust

113

you completely, trust your seriousness and discretion. . . . And your intelligence, naturally."

The intelligence of Cusan was, however, at that moment like a flooded motor. "I've come to report on everything that Rogas told me at that meeting."

"Do you mind if I make a tape of what you're going to tell me? For your own protection, so that those other persons may know exactly what part you had in the thing." He smiled. "This way, they'll leave you alone." And again he asked, "Do you mind?"

Cusan minded. And he did not understand. He said, "I don't mind."

The Vice-Secretary pressed a button on his desk. "There," he said.

Cusan began to talk. Insomnia and the anxiety of the last few days made his memory clear; he delivered a recapitulation of what he had written in the memorial hidden in *Don Quixote*.

When he had finished, the Vice-Secretary drummed nervously on his desk, staring at him with an indecipherable expression. Then he assumed an air of funereal solemnity and said, "Mr. Cusan . . ." A long pause. "What would you think, Mr. Cusan, if I told you that Amar was killed by your friend Rogas?"

As if a trap had opened before him. And, falling into it, he said, "Impossible."

The Vice-Secretary opened a drawer in the desk, pulled out some papers, pushed them toward Cusan, who mechanically picked them up.

"Read that," the Vice-Secretary said. But since Cusan, instead of reading, kept staring at him, he explained, "They are photocopies of the ballistic evaluation, autopsy, agents' reports, and of the statement made by the agent who killed Rogas."

"So Rogas actually was killed by an agent. As I suspected."

"Yes, but because Rogas had killed Amar."

"I can't believe that."

"Listen to me, Mr. Cusan. . . ." For Cusan sat as if lost in painful mental confusion. "Listen to me. Saturday morning, Rogas went to the Chamber of Representatives. He managed to approach Amar. He talked to him about a plot he had discovered. I do not know exactly what they said to each other. Amar merely told me that someone from the police had come to make some disclosures about a plot, and that they were to see each other again at the National Gallery. Our firsthand information stops here. Now the Center of Special Information enters the picture. For some time, on the basis of suspicions that unfortunately did not prove unfounded, they had been running a surveillance on Rogas—"

"But precisely because Rogas had got wind of the plot."

"Maybe. But the fact is that Rogas, and not one of the people in the plot, killed Amar."

"But why? . . . I mean, why do you believe Rogas killed Amar?"

"Because in the documents I've given you to read, there is a logic, a truth. . . . Amar was killed by the revolver that Rogas had in his hand when he in turn was killed. Trustworthy experts and some of our own Party people have verified this beyond any doubt. . . . You will think—and we also thought—that Rogas was killed first, and then came the *mise en scène*. . . . But it has been ascertained that there was only one agent from the Center of Special Information at the National Gallery, and he would have had to kill Rogas, take away his revolver, and then kill Amar. And Amar—what would Amar have been doing while the agent was removing the revolver from the dead Rogas's hand? Would he have waited for his turn? . . . He was a man of quick reflexes. You know, he'd fought with the Underground, he swam and played tennis regularly. He would have reacted, right? And in this case, for the agent to carry out the plan, he would have had to kill Rogas, strike Amar hard enough to stun him, take the revolver away from Rogas, shoot Amar. But no trace of a bruise or abrasion has been found on Amar's body. So then what? . . . Then we should have to grant that Rogas was an accomplice of the agent: that he killed Amar, not expecting to be killed in his turn."

"Impossible," Cusan said.

"We think so, too. But not out of regard for the memory of Rogas."

"I knew him well," Cusan said.

"Not well enough, Mr. Cusan. Not well enough."

"But why *would* he have killed Amar?"

"This we don't know. But he killed him."

"But what could Amar have said that would unhinge Rogas—"

"Mr. Cusan—" in a tone of sorrowful reproach.

"I mean to say, to unhinge Rogas, to drive him to do such a thing?"

"Look, your friend certainly did not care for us. . . ."

"No, I suppose not, but he made a fetish of opposition, and inasmuch as the Revolutionary Party is *the* opposition . . . He respected it, in a word. . . . And when he

116

talked with me, when I advised him to talk with Amar—advice that he surely expected from me—he said there was no other way."

"Indeed," the Vice-Secretary said ironically. "There was no other way: talk to Amar out of the mouth of a revolver."

"Incredible. Enough to drive one out of one's mind," Cusan said.

"Read the reports," the Vice-Secretary said.

Cusan read them.

"But why kill Rogas?" he demanded. "Why not hear him, put him on trial?"

"Reasons of State, Mr. Cusan. They still exist, as they did in the time of Richelieu. And in this case they coincided, let us say, with reasons of Party. . . . The agent made the wisest decision he could make: to kill Rogas, too."

"But reasons of Party— You— The lie, the truth—in short—" Cusan was stammering.

"We are realists, Mr. Cusan. We cannot run the risk of a revolution's breaking out." And he added, "Not at this moment."

"I understand," Cusan said. "Not at this moment."

NOTE

Just ten years ago, I contrived to stub my toe, as the saying goes, by appending a note to my book *Mafia Vendetta*. I had added that note by way of pointing to the moral of the fable: pretending, since I had written against the Mafia, to be afraid of the law—I afraid, whereas the Mafia were not. But most people took my note literally, and even today some reproach me for it.

Now I hope that this note will be understood as the other should not have been—literally, I mean. So: I wrote this parody (a comic travesty of a serious work that I had thought of writing but then did not write, a paradoxical utilization of a given technique and of current clichés), taking a news item as my point of departure. A man is accused of attempting to murder his wife; the charge is made on the basis of a concatenation of clues that, it seemed to me, might have been made up, prearranged, and supplied by the wife herself. Around this case, I sketched the story of a man who goes about killing judges, and of a police officer who, at a certain point, becomes the man's alter ego. An amusing pastime. But then I went off in a different direction for, at a certain point, the story began to unroll in an entirely imaginary country; a country where ideas no longer circulate, where principles—still proclaimed, still acclaimed—are made a daily mockery, where ideologies are reduced to policies in name only, in a party-politics game in which only power for the sake of power counts. I repeat: an imaginary country. One can think of it as being Italy; one can also think of it as being Sicily, but only in the sense in which my friend Guttuso is speaking when he says, "Even if I paint an apple, Sicily is there." The light . . . the color . . . And the worm that is eating the apple from within? Well, in this parody of mine the worm is entirely of the imagination. The light, the color (after all, is there any?), the incidents, the details—all can be Sicilian, Italian, but the substance (if there is any) must be that of a fable about power anywhere in the world, about power that, in the impenetrable form of a concatenation that we can roughly term *mafioso*, works steadily greater degradation. Lastly, I should add that I kept this fable in a drawer in my desk for more than two years. Why? I don't know, but this could be one explanation: I began to write it with amusement, and as I was finishing it I was no longer amused.

L. S.

73 74 75 76 77 10 9 8 7 6 5 4 3 2 1